D1369979

LIFE OF A
B**CH PT. 1

BY: TaKita Woodson

TABLE OF CONTENTS

This book is dedicated to my grandmother Rosemary E. Woodson R.I.H my love you are truly missed and I love you.

To my mother, who has always supported me through the good and the bad times. I love you Shirley J. Woodson.

To my sister and my brother, Angelique E. Woodson and Randall D. Woodson who are my #1 supporters and no matter what you have always been right by my side.

To my Aunt Winifred V. Sanford, who has always been a second mom to me. No matter what the situation was you were always there. I love you to the moon and back lady.

INTRO

My name is Tracie Burns. I was born December 12th in California, in the projects. Growing up I didn't have much, some days my sister Tania and I went to bed hungry and some day's cold. My mother Tonya Burns worked 24/7 trying to make ends meet and make sure my sister and I had a roof over our head. My dad split on us when I was 14 years old and Tania was 13. Left my mother with nothing not even a pot to piss in!

My mother is the strongest woman I know because she never showed that she was hurt, tired or even bitter! She always kept a smile on her face with her head held up high! My mother always taught us that you work hard for everything that you want and desire, never beg anyone for anything. She was a woman of pride and that no one, not even a man could take that from her. My sister Tania and I was very close while growing up. We were all that we had and my mother has always stretched that to us. My grandmother, my mother's mother was always a big help in our life, then she died when I was 15 years old. My mother took that hard. I had never seen my mother cry not even when her mother died.

Growing up Tania and I begin to grow distant from each other we did our own thing. When Tania was 14 she made my mother a grandmother, then again at the age of 15 and 16, but my mother made her abort all three babies. She made it even harder on our mother! When I graduated from high school a month later my mother died of cancer that she hid from Tay and I. We had nobody then, just us. I had to step up and take care of my sister. We stayed in my mother's' house as long as we could. By the age of 18 I was homeless living in a shelter with my sister.

Those poor days are over for me I'm 36 years old living in Beverly Hills and I drive a Lexus Truck. My sister Tania hates me; she thinks that I think I'm better than her but that's not the case. I promised myself when I left that shelter that I would never turn back, that I would never live that way again and for the past 18 years that's exactly what I've been doing! When I left high school, I started dancing at this low-key spot with my girl Lola. We danced for that crazy ass club for 6 years but I soon got tired of working a 9-5 and then going to the club from 10-3. I was worn out! So, I started my own little venture. I worked at a bank making pretty good money but not enough to get what I wanted and where I wanted, so I worked my 9-5 and did my own thing whenever and however I wanted.

Now some people may call me a hoe, a street worker, a prostitute but I don't see it that way. I fuck rich niggaz, rich bitchez, shit I fuck rich anything for money, cars, jewelry, or anything that has value to it! If I can flip it for a couple thousands, then I will let you fuck me for a couple minutes. I am not the average size woman I am a size 20 5'6 and proud as hell of it! I hold it in all the right spots; I have thick legs, thighs, 48DD breast and a round ass! Niggaz love me and Bitchez hate me, well at least

some.

CHAPTER 1

It's 5:10 p.m., I'm just now getting off work waiting

on Lola to come and pick me up. My car is in the shop, had

to get that candy-coated paint job. Lola pulls up with her music blasting in her night blue Trail Blazer. I start walking up to the door when this silly bitch decides that she want to TRY to make me chase the damn truck. I stand in the bank parking lot with my hand on my hip because there's no way in hell I'm about to chase after her ass…

Tracie: "Come on bitch stop playing I gotta be at the car shop at 5:30." She reverses back laughing like she was at a damn comedy show.

Lola: "Hoe stop crying and get ya fat ass in."

Now at this time it's 5:15 the shop is 30 minutes away from my job but believe me Lola will get us there in half time. We pull up in front of the shop at exactly 5:30 and Mr. Tony the owner of Tony's Paint and Automobile Detailing was standing in front of the building. Mr. Tony was about 6'1 55 years old and a damn pervert! He has always had his eye on me, he does his banking at my location and always waits for me to service him. He said he will give me a deal on my paint job, so I took it. I look up at him smile my beautiful smile and wave then I turn towards Lola...

Tracie: "Thanks hoe call you later." I opened the door and stepped down from the truck.

Tracie: "Hey Mr. Tony where's my baby?"

Mr. Tony: "I'm right here mama," he says while grinding his hips in a circle motion flashing his gums, shit this man has no teeth. I walked into the shop and I saw my car and smiled yelling,

Tracie: "O it is perfect, I love it!"

Mr. Tony: "I knew you would sexy."

Tracie: "How much do I owe you?" I asked while getting my credit card out my wallet.

Mr. Tony: "It's free if you can do something for me." I looked up I already knew that he was talking about giving him some pussy.

Tracie: "And what is that?" I asked in a sexy voice and my flirtiest smile. Shit say what you want I know his price is about $3,500 for this damn paint job, I can keep my money in my pocket. He starts walking up to me and placed his hands on my titties…

Mr. Tony: "I want some of you, you can pay me with by pleasing me, if you know what I mean."

Now, any stupid bitch would have turned him down and might have slap the shit out his old ugly ass but not me honey. A $3,500 paint job for free nigga please, a hoe gotta do what a hoe gotta do. So, I took his hand and placed it inside of my pants and bit my bottom lip.

Tracie: "Is this what you're referring to Mr. Tony?"

His eyes bucked and his mouth opened wide, I could feel his dick getting bigger. The ugly ones always have the huge dicks and Mr. Tony was one of them. He rubbed his finger over my clit and responded….

Mr. Tony: "Hell yea mama!" I lifted my head up to the sky and he started sucking on my neck all I could think of was a bleach bath after this. He lifted up and said to me,

Mr. Tony: "I'm about to make u flood this joint mama." I tried like hell not to laugh but I couldn't... I laughed my ass off.

Mr. Tony: "You think I'm joking, don't you? Don't let the old age fool you my dear, wait right here."

I wanted to run but I couldn't leave my car. I hate fucking old men, but love their money and expensive gifts. Mr. Tony came running back from the back with a blanket and a condom.

He laid the blanket out on the floor and guided me down to it. I sat up on the blanket and kicked my Dolce & Gabbana red bottom shoes off. He sat down on the blanket and started sucking on my titties and it felt damn good. I guess no teeth is something special. I loved to get my titties sucked and he knew exactly what to do. He took his long-wet tongue and rolled it around my right nipple while he messaged the left one with his index finger and his thumb making them stand at attention. He switched titties, gently nibbling on the left one and wiggling the right one in between his fingers. I liked it and it shocked the hell out of me. He pushed me back on the blanket and pulled my panties and my pants down, stuck his face in between my legs and sniffed my pussy.

Mr. Tony: "O yea baby smell like roses." he laughed

I rolled my eyes in my head like really!!! He then stroked my clit with his tongue. I moaned for more and he stroked more while pushing his two fingers inside me; I moaned a little louder.

Tracie: "Ssssss Tony" He mashed his face deeper into my wet pussy sucking my clit. I start scrumming over the blanket he pushed my thighs up higher, removed his fingers from my pussy and inserted his long thick tongue I instantly cummed in his mouth.

Mr. Tony: "Yea baby, feed me, mama." He continued moving his tongue in and out of my pussy and my body continued to shake uncontrollably. I moaned louder!

Tracie:" Yes oooo eat me, baby!" He pressed his nose against my clit while his tongue was inside my pussy moving his head wildly. Shit this was the fourth time that I have cum in his mouth I hope his old dick is just as good as his old tongue.

He climbed on top of me and removed the condom from the wrapper. I looked down and this old man was about 13 inches long oh my! He threw my legs up around his shoulder grabbed his dick and beat it against my wet pussy. He then pushed his dick inside me slowly stroking me "Mmmm," I moaned and he went deeper in "Ooh!" I moaned and he went faster and deeper in. I tried to bite my lip to keep from screaming out but it was to good and I couldn't hold it in. He was fucking me faster, his dick going in and out. I could hear his balls slapping me against my bottom ass cheek that always turns me on. He laid on top off me in a push up position, this old ass man is doing push ups inside my pussy. I yelled for more and he started moving up and down as fast as he could. Then he stopped and said,

Mr. Tony: "Flip your fat sexy ass over"

He instructed, so I turned over on all four without asking any questions. He rubbed my ass in a circular motion and then slapped my ass to see it jiggle. He laughed while sticking his dick in my ass hole. He had no damn mercy for the back door he grabbed my hips and moved me back and forward on his dick the more I screamed and moaned the deeper he went. The deeper he went the louder I yelled. He let my hips go and start smacking my ass while I juggled it on his dick

Mr. Tony: "Hell yea mama, ooh sweet mama!" he yelled out to me as he climaxed!

Mr. Tony stood up putting on his boxers and pants

Mr. Tony: "So, when are we going to do this again?" he asked me smiling like a kid in a candy store. I looked up at him while I was fastening my pants

Tracie: "What you mean again? This was an exchange; you have something else to exchange with me Mr. Tony?"

Mr. Tony: "Hell yea, this dick mama."

Tracie: "Naw I'm talking cash or something expensive; I can get dick anywhere babe."

Mr. Tony looked at me as if he was confused. I hoped like hell that he didn't think that this was going to be on a regular basis. I must get paid for my services. He walked up to me and grabbed himself,

Mr. Tony: "Not this dick mama." I laughed so hard.

Tracie: "Yes, dick, any dick, ya dick, his dick, her dick, I can get any time. I have to get paid Mr. Tony. You know what I'm saying?" He backed up and looked at me with disappointment on his face

Mr. Tony: "So you used me?" he said as he smiled an empty smile.

Tracie: "What?? Used you? You got pussy and I got my

car painted for free an even trade. So, no nigga I didn't use you, if you put money on this pussy then you will have some more of this, if not then shit, fuck some other rat that's around here for free. I gotta get paid I have bills and love expensive shit and if you can't understand that then sorry for ya Mr. Tony."

I drove my car out the garage waving at Mr. Tony while he flicked me off. I just laughed what the hell did he expect that I was going to fall in love? Never that shit, love is for the birds I never have been in love and never want to. I see how niggas do my sister and the way my father did my mother. What's the point of falling in love if all love going to do is hurt you? That's why I always say I don't love these hoes! Because I don't! That's how I'm going to keep it.

CHAPTER 2

I finally made it home to my three-bedroom condo, home sweet home. I love my house! I decked this bitch out the way that I wanted it with the help of these rich people and I so thanked them. When you walk in, it's a big ass hallway with a closet door on your right and 3 steps in front of you. When I have company, I always have them put their shoes and coats in the closet before walking up the stairs.

Take a trip up the three stairs look to the right you see my living room, white carpet, leather burgundy love seat with the couch and lazy boy chair to match with the square glass end tables with burgundy swirl legs and the coffee table in the middle of the floor made just like the end tables just bigger and longer. I have a little mini bar off to the side with only decorative bottles of wine and champagne.

Now, look to the left and you will see the huge marbled floor, dining room with a crystal chandelier hanging from the ceiling. The 8-seated glass table that sat in the middle of the dining room with 8 cushion swivel chairs and a fresh vase of white roses on the middle of the table as the center piece and white and gold plates and napkins to match with the gold ring around the napkins to keep the silverware from falling out; in addition to that sits the crystal glass on the side of each plate. In the right corner is the lovely bar that has every liquor, wine, and champagne that you can name. I am a drinker baby; I love my alcohol.

If you go through the double swinging doors it is the beautiful kitchen, also marbled floors with the island counter top and stove that sits in the middle of the floor against the wall sits my silver stainless fridge that sits next to the sink that's connected to the counter with the microwave built into the wall next to the cherry wood cabinet doors. I have a little cherry wood table that sits 4 people with a fresh bowl of fruit in the middle of the table.

Go out the single swing door in the back of the kitchen and it takes you into the hallway onto my white plush carpet. Walk about 6 steps down and you see the bathroom with a marbled Jacuzzi tub and a walk-in shower next to it. I love candles and they surround the Jacuzzi and the sink that sits in front of it. Walk out the bathroom, go to the right and there are my two precious rooms. The room on the left is my computer room. I do all my studying in this room believe it or not I'm in college for accounting I have 2 more years to go and I'm done maybe then I can leave my past behind me and start a normal life maybe! It's nothing in my office but built-in bookshelves that I had done myself and a cherry wood desk with a swivel around office chair the expensive kind, good to be comfortable while studying in front of a 48' computer set up on the desk. I had pictures of my mother my sister and her kids around the office.

My favorite room in the house is my bedroom just so damn indescribable. I love this room. My king-size bed with my rose color sheets and blanket on top, neatly made up, the floor mirror that lets me see my whole plus size body. I love my body and not too many big girls do but this is the body that got me where I am now and I love it. I have a big ass walk-in closet full of clothes and shoes all name brands like Gucci, Prada, D&B, Coach and whatever else you can name that cost a fortune and the good thing is I don't spend a penny on them just pussy. I have two dressers and two night stands full of fragrance and makeup. I have an extra bedroom in the back set up for guest even though I never let guest visit me.

I took a nice hot bubble and vinegar bath and just relaxed and sipped my Moet & Chandon Dom Perignon Oenotheque Rose Wine. My cell phone rang and I could tell by the ringer that it was my begging ass sister.

Tracie: "Not right now Tay," I whispered to myself as I'm hitting the ignore button on my IPhone. She calls back five more times even did a private call like I was not going to know that it was her.

Tracie: "What Tay?" I answered the phone irritated as hell with her.

Tay: "Damn bitch I'm happy to hear from you to."

Tracie: "Tay, I have had a long ass day and I'm trying to chill out if I didn't answer the phone the first time or call you right back then that mean I don't want to be bothered at this moment I will get back to you okay, bye." I disconnected her. She texts my phone…

Bitch you are so rude and don't give a fuck about nobody but your damn self I just needed to talk to my sister is that to fucking much to ask for? fuck you Tracie.

I just sat the phone down because she only calls when she wants money or something. I got out the bath and dried myself off, lotioned up and was about to call and confirm my appointment I had with Matthew Bridges, a rich fine ass white man who keeps my notes paid on my condo. He is married with 2 kids but fuck'em I don't know his bitch ass wife, so I don't care; shit I wouldn't care if I knew the bitch. I gotta eat too. But, before I could call him my second-best friend Joanna called. I answered the phone,

Tracie: "What up Jojo."

JoAnna: "Hey Trace praised the Lord that he gave you another day to live."

Tracie: "Jo, please don't start with that Godly shit okay not even in the mood."

JoAnna: "Trace you need to change ya life, give ya life over to the Lord. I keep having these dreams about you I'm scared for you."

I met Jo when I was in the shelter we started dancing together but she got saved and quit now she trying to save every fucking body else. JoAnna use to be addicted to crack, but she always handled her business. She slept around like I, but she gave that up for an honest living.

Tracie: "Jo I am fine I'm doing well even without your God; my dear, Tracie makes this happen not no damn God"

JoAnna: "Tracie I'm going to continue to pray for you and

ask the Lord to…" I hung up on her ass. I hate all that Godly talk and shit.

<u>CHAPTER 3</u>

I then called my appointment for tomorrow after work leaving him a voicemail he has an extra cell phone that his wife knows nothing about.

Tracie: "Hey white boy, this Jane we still on for tomorrow at the four Seasons Hotel, give me a call." I know yawl didn't think I gave them my real name, did yawl?

It's 5:20 pm and I'm on my way to meet Mr. Bridges at the Four seasons. I pull up and have them valet park my Lex. I went into the hotel, got the key from the front desk and went up to the room. My appointment is not until 6, but I wanted to get here early to get ready. I took off my casual 9-5 clothes took a quick shower and put on this red see thru teddi that Matthew likes so much with the nipples cut out of them. I lay across the bed and waited until he came in. It's now 7:30 and he's still not here, I hate when people stand me up. I start getting up to go put my clothes back on and I hear the door open

Matthew: "Where's my big teddy bear?" Matthew walking into the room with a big ass smile and some red roses in his hand

Matthew: "I'm so sorry baby I know I'm late and I know how you feel about lateness but I'm about to make it up to you sexy." I looked at him and smiled

Tracie: "Okay baby, I ran you some bath water go jump in and I'll be waiting for you." I kissed him on the cheek and he made his way into the bathroom.

Twenty minutes later he comes out dick on hard and a big ass smile on his face. I get up from the bed turn the TV off and made my way towards him.

Matthew: "Come to daddy big baby." I seductively danced walking towards him; when I made it to him I grabbed him by his hips and moved down slowly on him kissing him from his neck all the way down to his pink little dick. He never satisfied me but I always act like he did. I faked every moment of it and he never knows. I licked the head of his 4-inch dick sucking the tip of it and juggling his balls in my hand.

Matthew: "Yea do it baby make daddy cum" I took his dick and pushed it all in my mouth making my tongue wrap around it then his body begins to shake.

Matthew: "O yea baby suck that dick." I begin to suck and stroke faster until he cum in my mouth.

Matthew: "Baby get up on the bed in the position that daddy likes." I walked over to the bed, climbed on top and got in the doggie position and spread my legs as wide as I could. I put my finger under me and start stroking my clit…

Tracie: "Are you talking about this baby?"

Matthew: "O yea mama play with that black cat."

I start moaning because of myself and he strolls over to the bed and slaps my ass with both hands. He then takes both hands spread my ass checks and swipe his tongue in between my ass like he was swiping a credit card. Now this he could do and pretty damn well. He buried his face into my ass and start licking around my ass hole "Sssss mmmm!" was all that I could moan while he was making my ass his dinner. He ducked his head under my dripping pussy and begins sucking on my clit. I lowered my bottom onto his face so he can get a mouthful, minutes later I cum in his mouth. I lift up off him and he positioned me back in the doggystyle position. He entered me from the back and stroked one slow long full stroke and I felt nothing. I moaned just to please him.

Tracie: "Yea white boy, fuck that black pussy."

Matthew: "You want this white cock, don't you?"

Tracie: "Yes daddy, fuck the shit out of me."

Only if he could! His wife probably wouldn't care that he was cheating she probably doing the same damn thing with a nigga with a big dick that could satisfy her cause he damn sure couldn't. He starts stroking faster and faster my fake moaning got louder and louder.

Tracie: "Hell yea I'm about to cum inside my black Cat…Pooh, ooh yes baby yeaaaaaaa!" And just like that it was over! He laid on the bed breathing like he just did some shit.

Matthew: "Jane you can leave now I'm done. Your check is on the night stand my dear same time and place next week." I set up on the bed and start searching the room for my items. I reached over on the night stand for the check.

Tracie: "Sure baby anything else before I leave daddy?"

Matthew: "No you were great honey and I threw in a little extra for you." I immediately opened the check up and my eyes grew big. I turned to him and smiled at him

Tracie: "A little, this is a lot I appreciate it though."

Matthew: "Anything for my black Barbie and you deserved that buy yourself something nice."

The check was for $5000! Now my mortgage is

$2500 a month, he gave me an extra $2500 to go shopping with. I always just deposit the extra for any time that I decide that I want to give up this life, which will be after I finish school and get a good paying job, I think!

I arrived at my home at 11:00 p.m., as I was pulling into the gates I see my sister and her two nappy head ass kids standing at the gate. Right at that moment I wanted to back out the entrance way and keep going but it was a car behind me. I pressed the window pad to let the window down,

Tracie: "Tay what are you doing here?"

Tay: "Coming to see my big sis." She walks up to the car with her two kids and now that she has gotten closer I see that it's a third one on the way.

Tracie: "O my Tay are you serious, again?"

Tay: "Trace I don't need you judging me damn, can me and my kids get in?" I spoke without thinking.

Tracie: "What the hell for?"

She rolled her eyes

Tay: "Please Trace I need to talk to you"

Tracie: "Damn Tay, shit." The car behind me start honking their horn and I honked right back screaming out the window

Tracie: "Bitch wait you ain't in no damn hurry to get in the damn house."

I pulled up to the gate and showed my Community pass. The gate pulled opened and I drove through irritated as hell.

CHAPTER 4

What the hell was Tay doing here, I'm not about to give her ass no more money so she can fuck it up like she always does. Tay and I worked for the same bank before until she got fired for stealing money for one of her baby daddies. Tay was a very pretty woman and it would not be hard for her to get a rich nigga to cash her out. She was a size 16 no stomach, no stretch marks even after all these damn kids, pretty big brown eyes and a firm plump ass just like me. She just always went after these no-good drug dealers who love to beat the hell out of her.

We walked into the house I yelled at them even Tay as they were entering my home….

Tracie: "Take off ya shoes and coats and place them neatly in this closet and walk to the back to the kitchen." They all followed directions and me into the kitchen.

Tay: "Nice place sis see you remodeled."

Tracie: "Tay what are you doing here, what do you have to talk to me about that we couldn't talk about on the damn phone?"

Tay: "Damn Trace, you act like I'm not your damn sister like I can't come and visit you."

Tracie: "First off, it's 11 at night who the hell visit this late and the only time I hear from you is when you need money and I don't have no money so don't ask."

Tay: "Bitch I know you lying you're a fucking accounta you have money but that's not what I want."

My whole family thinks that I am an accountant at the bank but I'm not. They have no idea where I get my money from. I dropped out of school and had to start over but they don't know that I just told them I didn't go to graduation.

Tracie: "What the hell do you want Tay?"

She looked at me with this sad little puppy face.

Tay: "I need somewhere to stay."

Tracie: "O hell no not here Tay I'm sorry but you cannot stay here."

Tay: "Come on Trace my kids and I have nowhere to go, Troy put us out Trace please."

Tracie: "No Tay why can't you ever do what the fuck you have to do to keep a roof over ya kids head. You always pay for these no-good ass niggas then run to me to bail you out, not this time Tay you're on your on, you and they

cannot stay here with me, no way, no how, no siree." She looked at me with this cold look on her face and a tear dropped.

Tay: "I don't need you Tracie fuck you, me and them will get the hell out of ya life. You are supposed to be here for me; we are family you are my older sister, but I don't need you."

Tracie: "I don't have to be there every time for you. You are fucking grown Tay start acting like it. I'm your sister not your mother you killed our mother." Again, me not thinking before I spoke and before I knew it Tay had slapped me across my face and even though I deserved it I couldn't let her get away with it. So, I slapped her back and we start rumbling in my kitchen, while her kids crying screaming "Mama, mama stop." Tay could never beat me in fighting!

I stopped hitting her and backed up off her and she got off the floor and wiped the blood from her mouth

Tay: "Bitch you never have to worry about me or my kids. You stupid bitch; you forgot where the fuck you came from. This money went to ya fucking head, you dumb fat bitch. I hate you Tracie and I hope you die bitch." Tay stormed out the kitchen yanking her kids and running down the hall.

Tracie: Screaming down the hall "No Tay I never forgot where I came from I just don't want to go back and you and your problems not about to send me back there. Grow the fuck up and stop letting these niggas beat the hell out of you and taking those kids money. Bitch you will need me again, you will be back hoe and when you do I will slam that damn door in your face. You not about to be the death of me." Tay opened the door and closed it back turned around and stared at me

Tay: "You think I killed mama Tracie, uh I killed mama> You think mama didn't know about you being pregnant by Mr. Frank, the old fucking gym teacher that you fucked for

$500 Tracie? you think mama didn't know that you aborted that baby?" My heart dropped, my feelings were so hurt, and I always thought nobody knew about that.

Tay: "Mama knew Tracie. Mama never shed a fucking tear until that fucking day so stop trying to act like you are just so fucking innocent you nasty hoe, now choke on that bitch have a nice fucking life."

Tay walked out the door and slammed it behind her! I dropped down in the hallway crying with my head in my lap. No one was supposed to find out about that how did my mother find out? I was so ashamed and embarrassed all that time my mother knew and she said nothing to me but to Tay. I forced myself to get up and get in the shower I cried that whole night, I was so hurt by everything that Tay had said, but, now I know how she felt.

CHAPTER 5

It was Saturday, no work for me and I was so

happy, but at the same time, still depressed about what happened between my sister and I. Tonight was the night that Lola and I went to the ballers spot downtown and partied like it's 1999! Every weekend both of us would get dressed up from head to toe and get it in at club with all the rich men and the ladies. We pay $50 to get in the door and receive it right back by the end of the night plus more.

I was headed to my hair salon to get my hair done by one of the finest hair stylist in the world tricked out Ricki! He was the best, knew just how to make my naps feel like silk and I loved him for that. He was nowhere near cheap, I always get the usual a sew-in weave in that runs me $500, weave included. Love my weave! And he does lashes for $50, you can't even tell that they are fake. Everyone thinks I have beautiful lashes but only if they knew that Ricki can hook them bitches up and they last for a month and a half.

Ricki's shop was a day club, drinks and music I

loved going into his spot. It was so elegant and lavish. You walk in and get seen, no waiting four or five hours to get in a chair, the longest I have ever waited was 15 minutes. While you are getting, your hair hooked up you can sip on a glass of wine.

I also get my hands and feet done here to, by Ms. Sassy! She makes me feel like I'm walking on air and my hands feel like a newborn bottom and its $150. The massage that Brandon gives are unbelievable $100 an hour for a whole-body message and his facials are to die for and that's included. I pull in at the shop parking lot and get out the car hitting my alarm. I walk around to the shop door and Ricki greets me.

Ricki: "Darling how are you today?" he kisses me on both of my cheeks.

Tracie: "I'm okay diva how are you, loving that top Ms. Thang." Ricki snaps his finger.

Ricki: "You know the diva is always fire honey." I laughed

Tracie: "That's what I'm talking about baby."

Ricki: Laughing, "Come on here darling have a seat let's get started." I walk towards Ricki's chair, sit down and he puts the pink coat around my neck.

Ricki: "So boo, how things in the hills? Have you found that special someone or you just too busy with work right now?"

Tracie: "Now Ricki you know that I'm not looking for no man and his trouble right now, I'm just living this good life of mine." Ricki started putting a hot oil treatment in my hair.

Ricki: "Girl you need to start letting a man treat you like this and not you using ya hard working money." I laughed

Tracie: "Can't no nigga treat me like I treat myself!" Ricki braided my hair and then sewed in my weave.

Shortly after he did my lashes over and then I went to the back looking for Brandon, after last night I needed a massage. I spotted Brandon tall sexy yellow ass, I called out to him with a sexy smile on my face.

Tracie: "Don't you supposed to be working or something

sir?" Brandon turned around and smiled with those white

teeth.

Brandon: "I was waiting on you beautiful, you're my next

client."

Tracie: "Well I'm ready handsome." he pointed his head to

his massage room, when we made it in the room he gave

me a sheet and told me to strip. I took off my clothes, put

my hair up in a ponytail and lay across the table. Brandon

walked back in and locked the door. He took some oil and

started on my shoulders.

Brandon: "You are real tense baby, just relax." I did just

that. I closed my eyes and erased everything from my mind.

I could feel his hands move down my spine and he

massaged and oiled and massaged. He did my whole body

for an hour. I felt his finger move inside of me, I didn't

know what to do, it just felt so damn good. But, I knew that this was wrong he didn't ask me. Should I stop him? Fuck it I'm just not paying for this damn massage. I didn't hear his pants unzipped, I didn't even realize that he had his dick out, not till he pushed it inside of me and stroked me. I tried to jump up but he pushed my back down on to the bed...

Brandon: "Just relax Tracie you want this, just like I do."

He wasn't lying I been wanting Brandon for the longest just couldn't bring myself to ask him out. He doesn't look like the type to like big women anyway, so I just looked over him. He was a fantasy of mine. He stroked a long deep stroke and my pussy begged for more, I have never felt this wet before. He told me to sit up on the bed and scoot down to the end of it, he grabbed my titties put them in his mouth and leaned me back. He inserted his huge long yellow sexy dick inside of me and I silently moaned. He held me while he sucked on me and stroked inside of me.

My body begins to get warm, my pussy got wetter

and my body begins to shake. What the hell was going on?

He speeds up the pace just a little and I tried my best not to

scream. I bit my lip and that didn't work. I screamed out

"OOO my god!" An hour later it was over. I felt good, I

didn't feel nasty nor disgusted I felt good. The whole 3

hours I was in that room he fucked me slowly and

passionately, with his hands and his dick, something I had

never felt. He pulled up his pants and left the room. I got up

put on my clothes and walked out the room. I looked

around for him and he was nowhere in sight. I felt like I

needed to pay him for that so I paid $300. I left it at the

receptionist desk because I could not find him. I felt that he

was just embarrassed so he ran off. I left the shop before I

could get my nails and toes done because I didn't want to

run back into him. I will just head to the chinks nail salon.

<u>CHAPTER 6</u>

I went to the nail salon around the corner from my

house. I could not get Brandon off my mind. I have to
shake him he's not good for me. Then the nigga left before
I could say anything to him! Stop Tracie right now I
repeated over in my head.

Chinese Lady: "Fifty dollars' ma'am, ma'am, hello ma'am
fifty dollars" The Chinese man lady yelled at me as I was in
a daze about Brandon! I snapped out of it.

Tracie: "Damn okay, calm down." I reached into my purse
and pulled out three twenty dollar bills

Tracie: "Here you go keep the change" He bowed his head
at me.

I left the chinks shop and on my way to pick up
Lola to head to the mall to pick up an outfit for tonight.
Maybe this would get my mind off Brandon. Lola lived in
the hills too but, she had an apartment. Lola didn't like to
work she just had her niggas pay her bills and buy her
expensive things. I pulled up at the apartment and honked
my horn twice before I saw Lola making her way to the car.

Lola: "Hold ya horses Bitch I see you."

Tracie: "Well hurry the fuck up." Lola opened the door and stepped into the car and I pulled off while half her body was hanging out. She managed to jump in and close the door, I was laughing my ass off.

Lola: "Bitch you trying to kill me!" Lola yelled while laughing.

Tracie: "Naw bitch that's pay back." I looked at her and started laughing! Lola looked at me and screamed,

Lola: "Bitch you got your hair and nails done without me, and I bet you got Brandon fine ass to do ya massage didn't you, Tramp!" I smiled when she said Brandon name.

Tracie: "Bitch he did more than my massage." I looked at her and my face expression said 'if you only knew'. Lola looked puzzled at first then she opened her mouth wide

Lola: "Bitch did you fuck that boy?"

Tracie: "No Lola I didn't fuck that boy." I waited to see what she was going to say.

Lola: "So what the hell happened?"

Tracie: "That man fucked me."

Lola: "OMG What?"

I gave Lola all the details on our way to the mall, but I failed to tell her that I couldn't get this nigga out my head. I also told her about the fight my sister and I had and even though I didn't like what she said, I could always count on her to tell me the damn truth. Family meant everything to Lola, and she felt that I shouldn't have said all that I said to her and she would've slapped the fuck out of me too if she was Tay.

We were walking around the mall and I couldn't get Brandon and the way he fucked me out my head. Why did he do it with so much passion? Why did he run out the room? What the hell is wrong with me? I never thought about a client like this. But, Brandon wasn't even a damn client! I'm fucking losing it! Lola and I got our outfit and shoes and were leaving to go get dressed.

<u>CHAPTER 7</u>

We went back to my house; I hopped in the shower and got cleaned up. When I walked into my room Lola was already dressed! Lola was a plus size diva too! She was tall and thick with long hair red hair this week no weave needed but she changed the color of her hair so much you would think she wear weave, but it all was hers. She had a red and black Louis Vuitton jean outfit on with a red low cut shirt and some black red bottom boots. She looked nice and classy!

Tracie: "Awe don't you look nice." Lola laughed while looking at herself in the mirror.

Lola: "Bitch I look good, thank you."

She walked into the bathroom to apply her make-up and I shut the door to get dress. I put on a black Vixenz design jean one piece jumper with the boots to match. I sprayed on some Dolce and Gabbana perfume and was on my way.

We left the house around 11pm. The clubs don't get to jumping until 12 anyhow. It was an upscale club so they closed at 4am. We pulled up to the club and valet parked. We walked up to the door paid and strolled into the club. The Chapter Paradise was live! There were so many niggas, rich niggas. O my I felt like I was in paradise. I went straight to the bar and ordered my first drink.

Tracie: "A round of 1800 please."

Bartender: "$35"

Tracie: "I'm sorry make that two rounds."

12 shots for me and 12 for Lola that will start us off. The bartender set the shots on the bar, I gave him the cash and grabbed 2 shots, Lola took her first shot with a lemon, I just threw my first two back. Three minutes later our shots were gone and we was on the dance floor dancing with each other.

Two men not so cute walked up to us and asked

could they join. Lola pulled the tall well-built man close to her and start grinding on him. The short one about 5'8 walked up to me and start grinding on my ass. He whispered in my ear,

Lee: "My name is Lee what's yours beautiful?" I turned around to face him so that he could hear me,

Tracie: "My name is Kelly handsome." I smiled and dropped down low on him and came back up and whispered in his ear,

Tracie: "Are you here with anyone?" Like I really gave a damn.

Lee: "No baby just me and my manz."

Tracie: "That's cool what yawl doing after?"

Lee: "Hopefully I can do you after." I laughed.

Tracie: "Well I can make that come true for you."

Lee: "Really, let's go now then."

Tracie: "Now I know you didn't think it was going to be that damn easy?"

Lee: "Shit I was hoping so."

Tracie: "I have bills to pay boo if you can't help with that then you shouldn't waste yours or my precious time."

Lee: "Damn for real for some ass?"

Tracie: "For whatever you want, you can take it or leave it." He looked at me like he was shocked.

Lee: "How much you talking, money is not an object to me baby?"

I stopped dancing and looked at him.

Tracie: "Well damn, pay my house note for next month baller."

Lee: "What is that 5-600 dollars?" I looked up him like he was stupid.

Tracie: "Baby try 2500."

Lee: "Naw baby that's a little high for some ass."

Tracie: "You get whatever you want baby."

Lee: "So me and my mans can hit for…" I cut him off,

Tracie: "$2500, I'll give yawl a deal." He looked like a

baby in the candy store

Lee: "Okay let me go talk to my boy." He walked over to his man that was dancing with Lola. Lola walked over to me and ask did I seal the deal.

Tracie: "Yes, you know it."

Lola: "So did I, let's make them double it." I already knew what that meant I shook my head okay and stated to her that I needed another round. She reached into her bra and pulled out a hundred-dollar bill.

Tracie: "You go get the drinks and I'll go talk to the guys." I walked away from Lola heading towards the bar.

Tracie: "Excuse me bartender man can I get 2 more rounds please?"

Bartender: "70 ma'am." I paid him and turned around to see if I could see Lola.

Bartender: "Here you go ma'am have a nice night." I felt a hand on my shoulder, I turned around it was Lola and the two guys.

By now I had forgotten the short one name. I downed all 12 of my shots. The two guys that we were about to leave with bought another round for all four of us. Three damn shots ain't shit to me I'm already on my... I lost count. I know I was feeling really good and horney. We all walked out and I headed for valet to get my car.

<u>CHAPTER 8</u>

Lola and I followed the men to this little dinky motel about 15 minutes away from the club. We pulled up behind them and parked. The short guy went into the office and got the key. We walked into the room behind them and closed the door.

John: "Okay ladies let's get down to business." the taller man said whom name I found out while talking to him outside was John and his manz name is Lee, damn that's right.

Lola looked around the room in disgust

Lola: "We will get down to business when we get our money." Lee made a funny face.

Lee: "Damn yawl gone get paid. Yawl some money hungry hoes ain't yawl?"

This little short shit was already irritating the fuck out of me I walked up to him and showed him the little 22 in my tittie

Tracie: "You want what the fuck you want and we want what the fuck we asked for stop crying like a little bitch and pay."

He looked like he wanted to piss on himself. I always carry my little 22 on me just in case one of the niggaz tries to get out of line. Like this lil short dick bitch in front of me.

Lee: "Damn baby I was just joking, be easy beautiful."
Lola start laughing hard as hell and John cleared his throat before he started speaking.

John: "He just stupid mama. don't take it personal the

liquor got all of us tripping." I never took my eye off Lee, I started laughing and pushed him on the bed. He made me want to fuck him knowing that he was now scared of me.

Tracie: "Don't worry baby I'll be gentle, I just need money first."

He reached into his pocket and pulled out a clip of money and put it into my hand I stuck it in my pocket. I got up off him and turned to face Lola she was counting her money that John gave her that bitch didn't play about her money, drunk or not she was going to count her cash. I walked over to her, she put her money in her pocket and looked up at me and grabbed my head. She put her tongue in my mouth and kissed me. I grabbed a handful of her ass and squeezed. We stopped and looked at the fellows to see their reactions and just like I expected they were speechless.

I laughed and start undressing Lola as she untied my jumper from around my neck. My DD's fell out as soon as she untied it. Lola picked up one of my tits and start licking my nipple staring at the guys while I unzipped her pants. She took my titty out her mouth long enough to take off her pants, then plopped it back in.

John was starting to undress and Lee was already undressing stroking himself. I pushed Lola down in the chair got on my knees and spread her legs open. I stuck my tongue in between her legs and licked her clit. She signals for John and Lee to come and join us. She stuck john dick in her mouth and begin to suck it. Lee got behind me and put his dick inside of me. I was still eating Lola pussy as she was pulling on my hair.

Lola: "OOOO damn Kelly bitch yes!" Lola screamed out.

Lee tried to fuck me harder key word tried. Lola pulled John dick deeper in her mouth and held it there, juggling his balls in her hands watching his eyes roll to the back of his head and within minutes he cum in her mouth. Lola took John dick out her mouth and stood up. Lee pulled out of me after he cum, I stood up and Lola instructed me to lie on the bed.

I got up on the bed and laid back. Lola shoved her fingers up in my pussy and start sucking my clit and John and Lee were pulling on their dicks to get them back hard. Lola start climbing on top of me and begin to hump my pussy with her pussy. I was laughing because we really were bumping pussy. John came and stuck his dick inside Lola ass and was fucking her while she was on top of me. I grabbed her nipple and begin to suck on her. Lee shoved his dick into Lola's mouth pushing it and in out. After 10 minutes or so we all switched places. Lola start sucking on my nipples, John was in my pussy fucking the hell out of me with Lee in my ass and I was cumin. This orgy went on for another hour and then we all passed out on the bed.

John: "So ladies, when can we do this again? That was like the best sex I have ever had." John said with a smirk on his face! Lola and I looked at each other and at the same time we spoke

Lola & Tracie: "Whenever yawl have the money."

Lee: "Shit money is not an object with us." I was getting up off the bed to put my clothes back on.

Tracie: "Like we said anytime yawl want to pay that money, yawl can feel free to give us a call."

Lee: "We need a number um Kelly my dear."

Tracie: "Lee my number is 555-4521." Lee picked his phone up off the nightstand and entered the digits I gave him.

John: "Trust me we'll be calling."

Lola and I left the Motel after we got dress. I got into the car and pull out the money clip that Lee gave me and its $5000. He was so scared he gave me too much money! It's 6:25 a.m. and we are on our way home. What a night!

CHAPTER 9

I woke up at 2pm with a major hangover. I looked

at my cell phone and had 12 missed calls and 6 voicemails.
I called to listen to my voicemails. "Hello Tracie this
Joanne give me a call when you get this have a bless day
goodbye." "Tracie this Jo again, I talked to your sister call
me yawl need to straighten this mess out, that's your sister
God is very disappointed in both of you call me." Tay
always complained to Jojo about me like she was my damn
mama, I really don't feel like hearing the shit. "Hey sexy
this is Brandon from the shop sorry about the other day
please give me a call at 555-8945 can't wait to hear from
you." After I heard Brandon message I hung up. I held the
phone up to my chest "He called me!" I was so geeked. He
called me! I was getting ready to dial the number that he
left when my phone rang again. I picked up

Tracie: "Hello." The voice on the other end was a male.

Brandon: "Hello may I speak with Tracie."

After they started talking I realized that it was
Brandon; oh my he called me twice.

Tracie: "Speaking may I ask who's calling?" I was so geeked up my face felt like it was about to break. I was smiling so damn hard.

Brandon: "Hey sexy this is Brandon, I called you earlier but there was no answer. I hope you don't mind me calling you."

Tracie: "O no I don't I just want to ask how did you get my number?" Like I really gave a damn I wouldn't have cared if he came to my damn house.

Brandon: "I um please don't tell Ricki because I can lose my job, but I looked through his client book! I blushed knowing that he went through all that trouble just to talk to me, the man put his job on the line.

Tracie: "O ya secret is safe with me what made you call?"

Brandon: "Well, I wanted to apologize about yesterday I shouldn't have done what I did without asking you; I just got caught up in the moment I just wanted you so bad." I felt like screaming but a happy scream.

Tracie: "Brandon, yes you should have asked first and I really wasn't expecting that, but I enjoyed every minute of it… So why did you run out baby??"

Brandon: "I just knew that you went to tell." I laughed.

Tracie: "I'm a grown ass woman if anything I wouldn't have told I would've shot ya ass!" I laughed.

Tracie: "No I thought you were embarrassed by me that's why I left so fast. You run out the room so fast I thought you went to go hide from me."

Brandon: "Hide from you"? He laughed.

Brandon: "No sweetie, see I um didn't wear a condom and I kind of nutted all over myself so I left to go shower and change before anyone would notice."

Tracie: "Did you just say you didn't put on a condom?" I really didn't care I would have a baby by his sexy ass! 'What the hell are you talking about Tracie get your shit together,' I said to myself.

Brandon: "I'm sorry, I said I was caught in the moment."

We talked for 2 hours and planned a date for tonight and I couldn't wait. What was I going to wear? O shit I have to get my hair curled again. I called Ricki and asked him could he please squeeze me in for 6pm, I had to beg him but he finally gave in. I wanted to wear something sexy and at the same time classy. What the hell am I doing? I have never been on a date that wasn't being paid for sex. I never had to get ready for a date with a guy that I was truly into. What is going on with me? I called Lola for advice and maybe she could help me, hopefully! Lola answered the phone yelling into it

Lola: "What up bitch what you got up for today?"

Tracie: "I need your help and advice."

Lola: "What's up girl I'm all ears?" I told her how I was feeling about Brandon and that he called me and we planned a date and this ignorant bitch laughed at me.

Tracie: "It's not funny Larissa Berry." (That's Lola's real name.)

Lola: "I'm not laughing at you darling, I'm laughing because my bitch is in love, that's why you have all these feeling and that's why you felt that way after he fucked you Tracie Nikkole Burns you are in love." Lola continued to laugh and I just felt bad.

I am 36 years old and I promised myself that I would never fall in love with a man again. I only loved one man and he broke my heart. Never again would I be so damn stupid, so why would I fall in love now! I am enjoying my life, I love my life, fuck this I just won't love him. I control everything in my life, I'm pretty sure I can control this. I'm just going to call the date off. I called Brandon and he picked up the phone in his sexy deep voice

Brandon: "Hello sexy please don't say you're cancelling on me." (What the hell?)

Tracie: "What makes you think I'm cancelling?"

Brandon: "Ricki said you made an appointment for your hair and you have not made it here yet and you're always

20 minutes early for your appointments and plus it's an hour before the date." I was speechless, now what the hell was I going to do I didn't want to crush his feelings, so I made up a lie!

Tracie: "No I was not cancelling I was going to tell you that I wouldn't be ready till 9."

Brandon: "Okay good that gives me more time I have one more client okay see you soon sexy."

Tracie: "Bye dear." (Damnit I was stuck!)

Tracie: (talking to herself) "Why couldn't I call off the damn date? All shit you bitching up Tracie. Fuck it I'm going to go but I will not let myself have a good time. I can control this!" (I get in the shower and get ready to head to the shop.)

CHAPTER 10

I arrived at the shop at 7pm and Ricki was pissed at me

Ricki: "Ms. Tracie you are an hour late."

Tracie: "I'm so, so sorry Ricki I got caught in something please forgive me." I batted my lashes that he did yesterday and gave him the puppy eyes.

Ricki: "Alright lady, come on and get in the chair."

Tracie: "Thank you so much."

Ricki curled my hair in 30 minutes and I was out. I looked around for Brandon but I didn't see him. He was probably in the back with a client. I just walked out to my car and took off back to my house to get ready.

I got home and I looked thru my closet. I picked this red corset dress to wear with some leopard print stilettos. I lotion and oiled my body up and began to get dress. I loved this dress it made me look smaller and brought out my hips and ass. I applied my make up and walked out the bathroom. I heard my doorbell rang. I got up from the bed and rushed to the front door. I peeped out the peephole and it was Joanne. What the hell was she doing here! I hesitated to open the door but she had already heard me. I opened the door.

JoAnna: "O was you on your way out?" Joanne asked as she still made her way in the door. I slammed the door

Tracie: "Actually I was, what are you doing all the way over here Joanne?" Joanne looked at me up and down.

JoAnna: "Well since you won't answer my calls I decided to give you a little visit, your sister and her children is at my house sleeping on my floor, she is very hurt by the things that you said to her and you turning her around." I stopped Joanne in the middle of her statement

Tracie: "Jo I really don't care okay. I have a life to live and I don't have time to babysit no grown ass woman, now if you would excuse me I have a date to get ready for."

Jo looked at me like she really didn't care.

Joanna: "Trace that's your problem you only concerned about Tracie."

Tracie: "Who the fuck else am I supposed to be concerned

about not Tay was she concerned about my mother?"

JoAnna: "Stop it Trace it is not Tay fault that your mother passed away."

Tracie: "I know it's hers and God's fault."

JoAnna: "Now you have crossed the line Tracie, God took your mother home cause she was suffering he wanted her to be in a better place to watch over her children, so that they can be taken care of…"

Tracie: "What the hell ever Jo. God don't give a damn about me or my mother shit you either you still live in the damn projects. You worship him so damn much but he can't get you a better damn house."

JoAnna: "You selfish… Lord please hold my tongue! It isn't about houses and clothes Tracie it's about living and walking in the right path while we are here on this Earth. It's about the afterlife where would you end up at when your body dies uh Tracie? Where would your soul go Trace?"

Tracie: "I guess to hell."

JoAnna: "You know what Tracie I'm tired of trying to save you, go to hell alone Tracie. I'm done with you. I hope the Lord have mercy on your soul."

I opened the door for Joanne and she stormed out! I shut the door and walked up the steps when I heard my cell phone rang! I ran to the bedroom to answer it. What do you know it's my boo Brandon.

Tracie: "Hello sweetheart."

Brandon: "Hello darling, I'm pulling up now."

Tracie: "Okay, I'm on my way out." I grabbed my purse and shoes and walked to the front door. I was slipping my shoes on waiting for his horn when instead I got a knock at the door.

Tracie: "This bet not be Jo" I whispered to myself. I opened the door and it was Brandon standing there in a Gucci black suite with a dozen of white roses! I was speechless I couldn't say a word. He looked so damn good, better than he looked at the job.

Brandon: "These are for you." he said and smiled.

I took the roses smelled them and sat them on the antique table that I have in the hallway

Brandon: "Are you ready sweet heart, I know women say one time but they mean two hours later." I laughed as I wandered down the hall struggling to put my shoes on

Tracie: "Whatever, I am ready sir." He stretched his hand out to me, I put my hand on his and he led me out the door.

CHAPTER 11

We pulled up at this fancy restaurant that I had never been to. The valets come to the Hummer and guided us to the front door. This was one of these restaurants where you needed reservations. I was so impressed. We walked into the restaurant and were seated at the table. It was so beautiful! He pulled my seat out for me and I sat down. I have never had a man treat me like this, I would just fuck them and they pay me, never have any of them took me out on a date or treated me like a woman or a queen. We sat at the table for hours and hours talking and laughing. I was so into him. It was nice to have a man ask me about myself, about my life, about what I wanted.

I was so in trouble. What the hell was I doing? A nigga could never love me and treat me how I should be treated. Brandon could never love me if he ever finds out what I do and how I got the expensive things that I own. We got up from the table and were on our way back to my house. I have never let a nigga know where I stay at. Yet along come into my house! But, tonight I was breaking all the rules I wanted Brandon to fuck me like he did at the shop, but longer. We pulled up to my condo and he came around and opened my door for me. I got out the car and he walked me up to the door.

Brandon: "So this is the end of the night for us Ms. Tracie." I smiled as I unlocked my door.

Tracie: "It doesn't have to be, you can come in." Brandon hesitated for a brief second.

Brandon: "Naw I think we better call it a night." What the hell did he just turn me down!?

Tracie: "Okay then, good night Brandon." He leaned over and kissed me on my cheek.

Brandon: "Good night beautiful." I walked into my house and closed the door.

I had a good time with him. I wasn't even expecting that. I was happy, but confused at the same time why didn't he want to come in. I walked into the bathroom and begin taking off my makeup and clothes. After I got out the shower I went and laid down and dreamed of Brandon. I am in deep!

Monday morning and I'm at work thinking about Brandon. It's true what Lola said, that I was falling in love with him? How can I stop this? Maybe I would just ignore him for a couple days. It's 10 minutes before 5 and I can't wait to get out of here. I close my line and begin to count my money drawer down. I take it to the back and clocked out. Soon I walk out the door to get into my car my cell rings. I pick up the phone,

Tracie: "Hello."

Becky: "Hello Candy how are you?"

Tracie: "Hey Becky, I'm doing fine and you?"

Becky: "I will be if I can see you tonight." This is just what I need something to keep my mind off Brandon.

Tracie: "Yes, you can, is 8 good for you?"

Becky: "Make that 9 and meet me at the Hills Motel."

Tracie: "U got it, see you later."

I make it home, run me some bath water and go through my mail. My cell goes off again and it's Brandon, I ignore the call, as much as it bothered me I still went through with it. He called again and again I declined his ass. Then he left a message.

Brandon: "Hey Beautiful was just thinking about you

maybe we can hook up tonight give me a call back."

His voice sounded so sexy and I wanted to talk to him. I wanted to go out with him, I wanted to have fun without having sex! But my feelings are too strong for him and I don't love anyone. I gotta let him go. It's 8 and I'm finishing my make-up for my lil thing, thing tonight. Becky has money lots of money and I need the money to put down on this building that I'm about to get to start me a clothing store. I was excited about starting my own business. I start going back to school next week so with me working and fucking and school and getting this business started I have no time for Brandon anyway. I was making my way out the front door when my phone ring, it's Brandon again, I took a deep breath and declined the call once again and then two more times after. He then left another message.

Brandon: "Tracie what's going on you are not returning my calls did I do anything wrong last night? Call me please!"

He did nothing wrong and that's the problem he did everything right! I just manned up and walked out the door to my car.

<u>CHAPTER 12</u>

I arrived at the motel and called Becky for the room number. She told me to come to room 6. I walked up to the door and I knocked. Becky answered the door,

Becky: "Come on in babe."

I walked in and saw another white lady sitting in the corner sniffing cocaine. I never was down with that shit Becky always snorted before we fucked and after.

Becky: "Candy this is Linda she is a coworker of mine and she wants to join us tonight if that's okay with you?" I looked at the funny built older lady; she looked like she was in her late 40's.

Tracie: "Hello Linda and it's fine but you know my fee doubles for an extra." Linda snorted her line and looked up at me.

Linda: "It's no problem hun, I have the money right here."
Linda pulled out a knot of money all hundred dollar bills
and threw it on the bed.

Linda: "That's 1500 baby girl." she said to me wiping her
nose. I picked up the money, counted it and looked at
Becky.

Tracie: "Where's your half?"

Becky: "It's right here babe?"

She put the money and my hand and I begin to
count. Becky was a tall slender attractive white woman
with red hair and money. The business she was in she could
not tell them that she was gay or even had a little interest in
a woman, so she paid for sex. She loved black women. I
took my jacket off and sat on the bed. Becky turned the
lights off and I began to do a strip tease. She loved to see
my ass jiggle and my titties swing. I pulled my hip jeans
down to reveal my pink thong panties, I walked over to

Becky who was sitting on the edge of the bed, put my foot on top of the bed grabbed a handful of her hair and pushed her face into my pussy!

Becky: "Yeah baby work that shit!" Becky screamed out. I walked over to Linda who mouth was standing wide the fuck opened, took her hand and rubbed it between my pussy. I start unbutton her shirt and sucking on her little bitty titties. They were just like a man's. I felt bad for her.

Becky got off the bed and pushed her fingers inside my pussy. I unfastened Linda jeans and pulled her jeans and panties off. I instructed her to get on the bed and for Becky to start eating her pussy. They did just as I instructed. I got on top of Linda face and told her to eat! I never had head like this before. She ate my pussy better than a nigga which was no shocker to me. The bitches always eat better than these niggas.

Becky got up from Linda pussy to put on her strap on. She came back to the bed and stuck it inside Linda and

I leaned over to eat Linda pussy. At that moment Linda couldn't focus she was scrumming all over the bed and moaning really loud while Becky was pounding her pussy and I was licking her clit. Becky stopped and pulled her dildo out of Linda's wet pussy. I stopped and got on top of Becky's dildo and rode it like I was on a real dick. Linda sat on top of Becky's face so that Becky could eat her.

Again, we switched positions! Becky took off the strap and I attached it around my waist and stuck it inside Becky while Linda sucked the juice from her pink pussy. After two hours of fucking each other I put on my clothes and made my way home. Halfway home I turned my cell phone on and I had 3 voicemails. I checked them just knowing they were from Brandon and to my surprise they wasn't. Damnit did I really run him away? Why am I sweating it that's what I was trying to do anyhow? I pull up at my condo and I see Jo's car.

CHAPTER 13

Tracie: "What the hell is she doing here?"

I wanted to go back out the gates but was too tired to drive back out. These bitches always pop up at my damn house uninvited, I should move on their ass! I pulled up into my garage and got out the car, before I could get out the damn car here comes Jo!

JoAnna: "Trace we need to talk." I closed the car door and walked out the garage hitting the garage button on my key to let the door down.

Tracie: "Damn can I get in the damn house before the whole fucking neighborhood hear my business?"

JoAnna: "You have such a nasty attitude you need to check it." I kept walking to the door because at that time I wanted to slap the fuck out of her. I open the door and walked in wanting so bad to just close the door in her face.

Tracie: "What is it that you want Jo, I'm tired and ready to go to bed."

JoAnna: "Your sister is missing."

Tracie: "No she not; she's with her baby daddy."

JoAnna: "And how do u know that?"

Tracie: "Because she left a message on my phone, why are you so worried about Tania."

JoAnna: "And why are you not? That's your sister Trace, you need to stop this madness and welcome her in your arms before something bad happens to her. You need to help her and stop pushing her away from you."

Tracie: "Jo is you finish? I'm tired and I have to work in the morning, so can you please leave, thank you?" I walked to the door and opened it! Jo looked up at me and walked out the door onto the porch and turned and faced me.

JoAnna: "You are a heartless person and something bad is going to happen to you if you don't get on your knees and pray to God for forgiveness."

I smiled at Jo,

Tracie: "Goodnight Jo, have a nice night."

I slammed the door in Jo face and headed to the back to the bathroom to take a hot bath. The only thing I could think about is that fine man Brandon! O my goodness why can't I get this man off my mind. I want him so bad but I can't have him because of my own reasons. I went to sleep thinking about his sexy ass and just having one more night with him.

<u>CHAPTER 14</u>

I'm at work feeling good and looking good. Ten more minutes and I was heading home to meet up with Lola. I was so ready to go shopping. I could be in the worst mood, but money and buying expensive shit put me in the best mood ever. It's 5:15 and I'm walking out the bank to my car.

Brandon: "Tracie, wait up please." I turn around and Brandon is running to my car. I was so surprised about him coming up to my job.

Tracie: "Brandon what are you doing here?"

Brandon: "I wanted to see you, why haven't you returned my calls sweetie, did I do something to you, did I say something wrong to you what is wrong, don't you like me?" Why did he have to come with this? I was so caught off guard with this shit.

Tracie: "Brandon, no you did nothing wrong you were the perfect gentlemen"

Brandon: "So why are you ignoring me and pushing me away?"

Tracie: "It's not you babe it's..." He stopped me in the middle of my sentence.

Brandon: "Don't say that line to me Tracie, you are the perfect woman to me." I looked at him in shocked only if he knew that I was not perfect by any means!

Before I could say anything else he laid this big passionate kiss on me! I was so turned on! No man has ever kissed me. He looked me in my eyes and grabbed my hands.

Brandon: "Tracie I love you I never had a woman that made me feel like this, I know we only hooked up once but, I have always been attracted to you and I love massaging you and conversing with you, I love being around you and I love that you are an independent woman, that you hold your own. I love you Tracie and I will do anything to keep you around and make you see that I'm not trying to hurt you in no way. I just want to love you."

I had tears in my eyes. What the hell was happening, how could a man have feelings for me?"

Tracie: "Brandon you don't even know me."

Brandon: "I can get to know you, I know that you are a very beautiful person inside and out, I know that you love walks on the beach and reading and that you love to be independent and not depend on a nigga or anybody, I know that you love expensive items and that your mother died and you had to grow up fast I know that you was born

December 10 and you have never had a birthday party, the rest I can get to know, I want to get to know, I would love to get to know."

A tear fell from my eyes he remembered everything that I told him about me.

Tracie: "Brandon I…" I couldn't bring myself to tell him that I love him too! What if he turns out like these no good ass men that sleeps with me for money. They have wives and girlfriends and sometimes they have both what am I going to do.

Brandon: "Sweetie you don't have to say it right now but I know that you will feel the same way as time goes by just give me another chance."

Tracie: "You did nothing wrong, it's me."

Brandon: "I don't care whatever you're going through we will get threw it together I really want to be with you."

I smiled at him and kissed him.

Tracie: "I want to be with you too."

Brandon: "Well let's make this happen, I will not let you down Tracie, I love you so much. You are the only woman that I need and want, you are my soulmate my Goddess."

I stood there in disbelief how can a man ever love a woman? Every man and woman I know never works out because of the man cheating habits. Look at Jo, she all in my business and her husband sleeps around at strip clubs, where he met Mrs. Joanna. I want to give it a shot but I am so scared every person that I loved deeply hurt me or left me. What to do, what to do? I think I had just invited him to be my man though! O my goodness I did! We went separate ways, Brandon ran back to his car and I got into my car with tears rolling down my face. I started my car and drove home.

I walked onto the porch and took the mail out of the mailbox; I opened the door with my key and walked in. I was going through the mail when I found a letter addressed from Ralph Luckett, it's my dad! How in the hell did he find me? I opened the letter and begin to read:

Dear baby girls,

I know that it's been years since the last time I saw you, talked to you or even held you. I miss you both and I love you girls with all my heart. I was sad when I heard about your mother. That was my heart, Tonya meant everything to me and more. I left because of problems that your mother and I had and you girls was too young to understand what was going on. I know that I shouldn't have left without saying good bye and that I shouldn't have never walked out of you girls' life. I was foolish back then and had a lot of things going on. I finally found an address for you girls, well for my Tracie, I could never find an address for Tania. I just need you girls to forgive me and I want to meet with you both one day and just set some things straight about your mother and I and Tania even though you're not

mine baby I always loved you and will never stop!

Please girls just give me a chance and come and see me

or I could come to you girls call or write back Love you

both! 323-555-8596

Father Ralph Luckett

What the hell he means even though Tania is not

his? What damn problems did he and my mother have? He

left my mother there to raise two damn kids on her own.

This mothafucker! Yea, I want to talk to him to give the

bitch a piece of my damn mind. Bitch! When I calmed

down I called Tania and read the letter to her.

Tay: "What he means that I'm not his Tracie?"

Tracie: "How will I know Tania?"

It was a long pause, a deadly silence between the

both of us. I had to say something but didn't know what to

say but she did.

Tay: "Is this mothafucker trying to say that ma cheated on him?"

Tracie: "Yes Tania"

Tay: "Tracie please let's go to his house and give this mothafucker a piece of our mind how the fuck he gone say that I'm not is, that's why he always liked you better or maybe because…"

Tracie: "Because what bitch don't say no stupid shit?"

Tay: "Tracie you remember when dad came back to see us when we were about 13 and 14?"

Tracie: "I don't recall the bitch coming back at all."

Tay: "Tracie, yes you do."

Tracie: "How the fuck you gone tell me Tania that's why I don't like fucking talking to you, you just fucking stupid."

Tay: "You are a piece of work you know that? Think all the way back till when u started selling your ass?"

After that Tania hang up and wouldn't answer the phone. I sat there all night trying to think about what the hell she was talking about. I don't know, I can't even remember that year at all. It's like it was erased from my memory. Why can't I think to when I was 14? I called Tania all night that night and she never answered. The whole time I talked to Brandon on the phone was the first time that I was not paying any attention to him. What the hell, remember Tracie!

Why can't I fucking remember? It was 2:25 a.m. and I still was up and had not had a bit of sleep I kept looking at that letter that Ralph wrote and I decided to call him and ask him did he come over when I was 14 and what the hell happened? Then I started thinking, did this bitch rape me? I dialed his number and then hung up. I want to know but was too fucking afraid! I dialed again the phone rang twice and I hung up.

Tracie: You can do this Trace just call the bastard and ask him what the hell happened… (She picks up the phone and hangs back up) I can't go through with this I don't want to know! I'm lying yes, I do!

While I'm sitting there contemplating whether if I want to know, my phone rang! It was Tania! I answered never been happier to hear from her this shit was racking my brain.

Tracie: "Tania please what happened, I can't remember."

Tay: "Tracie I don't want to tell you over the phone, maybe we should go pay Ralph a visit and you should talk to him."

Tracie: "Why can't you tell me Tania? Did he rape me Tania?"

Tay: "Tracie go see him."

After she said that I had set it in my mind that Ralph had took my innocent! At the moment I decided to take off work tomorrow and go pay Mr. Ralph a visit. Then I changed my mind I don't want to see him I can't remember and really don't want to. I was so mad and angry I cried that whole night! Why couldn't I remember? I didn't get up to go to work, I just slept in the bed all day and cried and ignored everyone. My life was more painful than I thought it was. I got raped by my father. What the fuck?

CHAPTER 15

I called Lola and told her everything that was happening. I was in love for the first time and was scared as hell about it. That the father that I thought Tania and I shared was just my father and that I was raped by my father. I was so stressed from this and I had to call my shrink so that she could figure this shit out for me. I pay the bitch enough! I made a phone call to her and set up an appointment for tomorrow. I was so going to see this expensive bitch but before I did I had to go make extra money.

Lola set up this party for us tonight at the Millionaire Merchant to dance with the ballers. I would have been crazy to pass this opportunity up. All the girls get tipped very well, all the men tip no less than $100 and private dances are $300 and up, depends on what you want.

Now my private dances consist of sucking and fucking, so baby I'm doing G's for each private dance.

Lola and I headed to the stripper's favorite spot HOLLYWOOD to get outfits for tonight. I had already made my hair and nail appointment at Ricki's. We get the outfits and shoes and now we're on our way to Ricki's. I was excited about doing this party because it was a lot of money involved and I would have enough to pay for this damn shrink and put some money towards my building for the clothing store. I wouldn't have to dip into my account to pay shit. The only thing that was bothering me about it was Brandon. I have a boyfriend now, should I still be getting down like this? Fuck it Brandon can't pay for my expensive habits and my problems. So, a woman got to do what a woman got to do! You feel me!

We arrive at Ricki's and Lola takes the chair first and I go to the back to find my man. That feels good to say my man! I laughed at myself. When I get to the back,

Renee, the receptionist was telling me that he had someone on the table. I stood there waiting but the only thing that was flowing through my head was what was he doing with his patient? Was he fucking her too? I began to get this pain in my stomach!

I wanted to know so bad what in the hell was going on inside that room. I told Renee that I had to use the little girls room and I started walking to the back. I looked behind me to see if Renee was paying attention to me and like always she was not, her eyes was on her mini television and her ear pressed on her cell phone. I turned around and walked into the direction of his massaging room and just as I was about to turn the doorknob, Brandon opened the door.

Brandon: "Hey baby what are you doing here?" I stood there with my eyebrow lift and my hand on my hip.

Tracie: "Why are you so damn shocked to see me?"

Brandon: "Baby I opened my door and here you stand,

then I had no clue that you was coming today that's all." I looked at him and rolled my eyes and yelled at him

Tracie: "Right Brandon, if you say so; was you fucking her like you fucked me?" He grabbed me by my arm and pulled me to the side. He whispered to me in an angry voice…

Brandon: "What the hell is wrong with you, I was working, doing my fucking job! Are you trying to get me fired? Did you come up here to spy on me?" I laughed at him and rolled my head.

Tracie: "Ya ass just got busted you know what I knew you was just like...." As I was about to tear him a new asshole his massage room door opened and a white older man walked out the room and waved at Brandon

Old Man: "Thanks son see you again next month."
Brandon forced a smile on his face and waved

Brandon: "See you later Mr. Tremble!" I put my head down I felt like a jackass. Why was I so stupid! Brandon looked back at me.

Brandon: "That's who you swear I was fucking." I couldn't say nothing, he looked at me with anger.

Brandon: "I have work to do I'll call you later."

Tracie: "Brandon wait let me explain." He turned around and pointed his finger at me...

Brandon: "Not here Tracie not at my fucking job, I have work to do; good fucking day."

He walked off into the back of the shop and I walked off back to the front. I felt stupid and hurt. What did I make a big ass scene for? When I got back to the front Ricki was done curling Lola hair and it was my turn to sit in the chair. My excitement for the night had gone. I wanted to talk to Brandon, I had text his phone and called but he wouldn't respond or answer. He hates me now! I knew couldn't no man love me!

After two hours of sitting in Ricki's chair my hair was finished. I paid him and Lola and I was on our way to her house to get ready for the night. The car ride home I was silent and I was in a zone. We arrived at her large two-bedroom apartment and started getting ready for the party Lola put on this pink lace thong teddy and some pink thigh boots. She looked so sexy in her lil pink teddy!

She started applying her makeup while I got dressed in my black see through lace thong teddy. My outfit lifts up my titties but had no cloth for the tittie. My titties were just out in the opening. But I had a black pea coat that I was wearing over it. I had some black thigh boots with the lace going up the side of the boot. I applied my make up in her bathroom and tried to call Brandon one more time. He pushed me straight to the voicemail.

Tracie: "Hello can you please call me when you get this I'm sorry about earlier please let me make it up to you okay, talk to you later I hope."

CHAPTER 16

I was in no mood to dance but I had to get myself

together. When we left Lola's house we went to the liquor store and bought a gallon of Hennessy and called my boy Jay to get some E pills. We met him at the liquor store and bought 4 double stacks we took 2 apiece. By the time, we arrived at the party we only had a pint of Hennessy left in a gallon bottle.

I felt so good walking into the party. We got checked in and they took us to the back so that we could come out on the stage and dance. Lola had pulled some strings and got us some time alone on the stage. We were going to do one of the old numbers but we had added a little more extra grown shit into the performance. They called our name and I'm like so nervous right now, I haven't danced in front of a crowd in so long.

We hear the song Bump and Grind by R. Kelly come blasting out the speakers. Lola and I took one more shot and then went up on the stage. Lola went left and I went right. It was so many fine ass men in that house. I was so turned on and the smell of money in the air made me even more aroused. I started dancing to the music in my pea coat and a man yelled to me "Baby take it off," then another "Yea baby show daddy what you got," I laughed and said…

Tracie: "Yawl want me to take it off?"

They screamed "Hell yea!" I laughed.

Tracie: "Then show us some love."

I turned around bent over and made my ass clap. I saw money flying up on the stage. I untied my belt and put it around this man neck, he smiled at me and then threw $100 up on the stage. I squatted down in front of him and put his hand inside my coat so that he could get a feel. All the men start roaring!

The man smiled from ear to ear. I returned to the center of the stage and unbutton my coat and let it fall to the ground. The men went crazy. My titties was out and standing up at attention. I continued to dance until the song stopped coming out the speakers. Lola and I grabbed our coats and money and walked off the stage. I made $2000 just by dancing. Kim the hostess came to the back handed me a letter from one of the guys at the party. The letter read.

I liked what I saw I want to taste you and feel the inside of you please take me up on my offer of $5,000 for one night with you! -Kevin Hill Jr.

Hell, yea I was going to take him up on this offer! $5,000 to fuck him? I damn sure would! I wrote back on the letter yes meet me in the private room area! I gave the letter back to Kim so that she could pass it along! I wanted to know how this rich nigga looked. The private dances started at midnight and I went into the room I was assigned and in there sat this chocolate smooth skin, deep waves, sexy ass brother with a tailored Prada black suite on and some black gators. I was not expecting this! This man was fine as all hell. I smiled

Tracie: "Hello are you Kevin?"

He sipped his drink and said in a smooth deep sexy voice replied…

Kevin: "Yes sexy lady, in fact I am."

He stood up and was every bit of 6'4, I wanted him so damn bad at that moment I couldn't even tell you who the hell, damn what is his name…O yea Brandon was! I was so ready to fuck the shit out of him! Kim the host swipes the credit cards and takes all cash before the man is even allowed in the rooms. She takes a portion of her money and the rest goes to the women. Since he offered $5,000 I knew that I was only getting $4,000 back and this man paid with cash so I knew that I had to fuck him good. He walked over to me and took my hand bent down and kissed it.

Kevin: "How are you doing this evening my lovely Queen?"

I was so into him.

Tracie: "I am fine baby, ready to please you."

Kevin: "Is that right, dance for me mama let me see you move that beautiful body of yours."

I walked over to the stereo that was in the corner of the room and turned it on. Usher "Can you handle it?" came bursting out the speakers. I downed 2 shots of 1800 before I started to dance. I start moving my hips to the beat and feeling on myself. Kevin sat in the chair over to the side watching and sipping his drink. I walked over to him and straddled him; I got the rhythm of the music and start bouncing my ass up and down like I was fucking him. I threw my leg around his neck and sat frontwards on his lap.

I took his arms and wrapped them around me and began to grind on his erect dick. I slide on the floor into the splits and start rolling my ass around on the floor. I got up off the floor still feeling this Usher song the liquor and pills from earlier. I was so into this song dancing my ass off. Kevin walked up behind me and bent me over. He rammed his dick into my ass and put his hand over my mouth. I screamed he was hurting me; this was the first time a nigga ever treated me like I was a piece of meat. I felt violated.

He threw me on the bed and jumped on top of me! He whispered to me "You a hoe bitch and that's exactly how I'm about to treat you" I tried to scream but before I knew it he punched me in my face with full force. I was knocked the fuck out! When I woke up I was tied down to the bed and had tape over my mouth. I looked around the room and saw him sitting in the chair smoking a cigar. I started making noises and wiggling trying my best to get up! He got up from his seat and walked over to me. I was scared, crying my heart out! Why is this man doing this to me? He whispered in my ear and said…

Kevin: "You ruined my damn life, you stupid bitch and I'm here to end yours."

I closed my eyes tight and I start shouting knowing that no one could here. He looked me in my eyes and laughed.

Kevin: "Well your time's up Bitch!"

I was so scared; my heart was beating like a drummer and my adrenaline was really rushing. I could feel my veins coming out of my body.

He punched me again and again until I was unconscious. When I gained, conscious back I was laid up in Memorial Hospital bed with Brandon, Lola, Jo and Tania surrounding my bedside. I felt sore and tired. My whole body ached, I couldn't move. I looked at Brandon and started crying! Did he know what happened? What have they told him? Brandon walked to the head of the bed and grabbed my hand.

Brandon: "Don't cry baby we going to find the nigga who did this shit to you."

I looked over at Lola and she winked. That lets me know that she made up a lie about the incident. Tania came and grabbed my other hand.

Tay: "Sis don't worry just rest and get better, whoever this mugger was the police better find them before I do."

Mugger? Lola told them I got mugged! Okay good one I looked at her and tried to smile.

Lola: (crying) "I just can't see her like this."

And ran out the room. Tania went after her. I looked at Jo and muttered…

Tracie: "I want to see my face."

Brandon looked at me with concern on his face.

Brandon: "Baby, not now I don't think you're ready."

I looked up at him.

Tracie: "I want to see my face."

Jo and Brandon looked at each other and then the door opened, Tania and Lola was walking back in the room. Lola walked up to me and kissed me on my forehead. I whispered to her.

Tracie: "I want to see my face."

She looked at Brandon.

Lola: "Trace you just need to get rest and don't worry about ya face right now."

My voice got deeper and louder...

Tracie: "Damnit, I want to see my fucking face."

Tania dropped a tear and walked over to her purse and pulled out a mirror. I opened the mirror up and I screamed and cried. I threw the mirror and told everybody to get out.

Tracie: "Get out all yawl just leave me the fuck alone...Get out... leave."

Nobody moved. Brandon hugged me and I tried to push him off, but I couldn't. I wasn't strong enough to move nothing. So I just let him hold me and cried on his shoulder. My face was fucked up. I had stitches going down my face, two black eyes, swollen lips and nose and scratches on my face. I was hurt. My looks are what get me by. And this bitch ass nigga took that from me. What the hell did I ever do to this man, I don't even know him. I remembered he kept saying to me bitch you ruined my life. How? I don't know him?

The police came into the room and told everyone to leave out besides Lola because she was at the Chapter. The police questioned us for two hours and assured me that they were going to find the man that did this. I hope so cause if I ever see this bastard before they do, I swear on my mother I'm going to kill him. I could not stop thinking about what he said to me before he beat the hell of me **"Bitch you ruined my life!"** What in the hell was he talking about? Why would this man pay for me to fuck him then he beats me up and takes nothing? All my belongings were still in the room. I don't understand what the hell has happened. I just want to go home but the doctor is keeping me for a couple days.

What the hell have I gotten myself into. When I go to the bathroom, I don't even look at the mirror. I can't look at myself. I look so damn ugly. I look scary like I just came out of a damn scary movie.

CHAPTER 17

I was finally home from the hospital. Tania decided that she would stay with me to help me out around the house. I was depressed and sad. Brandon tried to get me to stay at his home with him, but I just wanted to come to my own house. Tania was so excited because she got a chance to drive the Lexus for the very first time. No one ever drove my car and she felt honored. We pulled up to the condo into the garage and enter the house, she was so happy to move in and in a way, I was too because I was scared to be alone. Tania set up her things in the guest bedroom. That night for the first time in life my little sister and I had a heart to heart talk. We laughed, we cried, and we shared stories. I just couldn't bring myself to tell her where all my things came from.

Tay: "You know Trace I look up to you, we both came

from the same household, same neighborhood and had the same opportunities and I fucked up. I picked these dead beat ass men instead of going to college like you did and doing something with my life. You have it made, you have a beautiful life, nice house, car, great paying job and you have no kids and a sexy ass man…"

She paused and start laughing.

Tay: "Yes, sexy man."

She sipped her drink and rubbed my hand.

Tay: "Thank you Tracie for being a mother to me when our mother died. I'm jealous of you and that's why I fight with you so much."

I looked at Tania in disbelief; she has never told me things like this and it was nice to hear. No one has ever said congratulations or thank you for growing up and taking care of our family. It was always something negative and that's why I cut my entire family off and just said fuck'em. I couldn't believe my sister was expressing her feelings to me it's the alcohol talking, but I liked this side of her.

Tracie: "Tania I love you that's why when I cut the whole damn family off, I never cut you off and sometimes you get on my damn nerves."

We both laughed.

Tracie: "But, I will always be there for you when you need something, I wouldn't let you move in with me because I just thought that you and the brat pack would be in my way and that I would get close to…"

I stopped and looked her and her eyes.

Tracie: "Someone that I really cared about and that you would fuck over me like all the other stupid bitches and these grimy ass niggas. That's why I always look over you or just go full blast on you! And bitch please don't be jealous of me my life, it is not what it seems"

Tay: "Well Trace from the way it looks your life is great. I want to be like you when I grow up! (pause sips drink) Lola and you are real close why can't I, your sister be that close to you, why can't we bond like you and Lola?"

She made a good point why would I open up to Lola and not my own damn blood? I just sat there and pondered that question!

Tracie: "We will make that bond Tania closer than Lola and mines."

She looked up at me as she was sitting the glass on the coaster.

Tay: "Are you serious Tracie I hope this just not the liquor talking I really want a relationship with my one and only sister."

I put my hand on hers.

Tracie: "You will Tania you will!"

We both smiled!

Tracie: "Tania what happened that summer with daddy"

Tania stopped in her movements and looked at me like she saw a ghost.

Tay: "You really don't remember that night do you Trace?

You pushed it out ya mind! Maybe it should stay out ya mind."

Tracie: "No Tania, I need to know maybe that will explain me not being able to sleep at night, the tossing and turning and it might explain why I have issues when it comes to love and why I be so damn mad all the time and why I just feel like it's me against the damn world; what happened to me Tania?"

Tay: "Tracie I can't do this, I can't bring myself to hurt you like that."

Tracie: "Did Ralph touch me Tania?"

Tay looked at me and shook her head.

Tay: "No not Ralph."

Tracie: "Then what the hell happened Tania tell me please."

Tay: "Okay Tracie I'll tell you, but I don't want to. Maybe you need to finish healing first."

I looked her in her eyes and tears start falling from

mine.

Tracie: "Tania I need to know right now."

Tania moved around in her seat.

Tay: "Tracie you erased like 2 years out your life, I knew that Ralph was not my father, mama had messed around with a man name Kevin he was dad's best friend, well anyway mom and Kevin had an affair that's when I was born. Dad was in the army, so there's no way that he could have made me so he dipped on her. She begged him to come back, he did but mom was still sleeping with Kevin. She was in love with Kevin but Ralph had money; mama stringed Ralph along for the money.

When you was about 12, Kevin start noticing your shape. He always said little things to mama about it, she did nothing because she wanted him to stay around so one night he crept in ya room and he…he, he touched you he held you down and raped you and mama was standing in the door looking and crying, but she didn't stop him. She was in love with him and she did nothing."

I sat there amazed, shocked, hurt, sad, and alone. I looked up to my mother and this bitch, this bitch let her man take my innocents from me? I couldn't talk, I couldn't move.

Tay: "This went on for a year and one day mama was in the bedroom reading a book like everything was just normal knowing that Kevin was in her daughter room having his way with her she did nothing, she let it happen it was either you or Kevin."

A tear fell from Tania eyes she caught her breath and continued the story.

Tay: "Ralph came home early I let him in and told him to be real quiet. I snuck him upstairs into your bedroom, when Ralph opened the door Kevin was on top of you and you was crying "Stop please stop!" Ralph dropped his bags and ran fast over to your bed and beat the shit out of him, mama came running down the hall screaming "What are you doing? Ralph stop this now get off him," and she start beating him in the back, I came and put the cover over you, you were on the bed shaking so hard. Ralph stopped hitting Kevin when Kevin stopped moving. He looked at you with tears in his eyes and said I'm so sorry baby girl I'm sorry! Mama called the police on Ralph but before the police got there ralph took off. I wanted to tell but mama said if I did that she would beat me. Mama continued to be with Kevin until that one summer night."

Tracie: "What happened that night?"

Tania looked at me and more tears rolled down her face.

Tay: "Mama wanted Ralph back because Ralph kept the bills paid but the only reason he came back around was to keep his eyes on you. Kevin came back one night when Ralph wasn't there, now Ralph gave me his job number and his pager number to call him if he ever showed back up and I did. This time when Ralph caught him he killed him, one gun shot straight to the head and he beat the hell out of mama, he sat there until the police came he got 10 years for killing a man and beating mama unconscious. Your dad loved you Tracie, I gave him your address, I talk to him every other day about you, he was up at the hospital but I made him leave before you woke up. You worshipped mama so much and I never knew why but I do now because you erased those years out your mind, I always knew why you were so heartless I couldn't blame you!"

I was hurt my own mother, I hated my father but I would give my last to my mother. I hated Tania because I have always had it set in my mind that she was the cause of my mother's death, I was so wrong, I hated the two people that loved me the most and I loved the person that hurt me the most. I went into my room and cried! Kevin was Tania's dad and her dad Kevin... Hold up Kevin.... Kevin is the dude who beat me. I jumped up out the bed and ran into the guest room busting the door open...

Tracie: "Tania! Tania!"

Tania jumped up and grabbed the little white pistol that she carried for hers and her girl's safety, she ran to the door and I grabbed her.

Tracie: "No, wait what the hell are you doing?"

Tay: "Bitch you screaming my name like somebody came in this bitch. What is it?"

Tracie: "What was Kevin's last name?"

She looked at me and starched her head.

Tay: "I don't remember."

Tracie: "Tania, yes you do. Please remember what his last name was."

She stood there thinking hard.

Tay: "O it was Hill."

I just dropped right there in my hallway **KEVIN HILL JR.** was the name that was on the invite the sexy well-built man was Kevin Hill's son. I couldn't tell Tania because I would have to tell her about the incident. She got on her knees and removed my hands from my face.

Tay: "What's wrong Trace, do you remember now?"

I had to make up a lie or I could just snap on her.

Tracie: "No, just get away from me."

I jumped up and run into my room. How in the hell did he know it was me, how did he know that I was going to be there that night? I was afraid for my damn life now! Was he trying to leave me for dead or was he trying to make me suffer? I couldn't sleep. I got up the next morning and went into the bathroom to take a nice hot shower.

CHAPTER 18

I could smell breakfast coming from the kitchen. I got out the shower dried off and put on my robe. I walked towards the kitchen thinking, how in the hell did Tania cook? I don't keep food in the house because I am never here to cook and eat. I haven't had a good home cooked meal in a long time. I walked into the kitchen and Jo was mixing eggs, Tania was frying bacon and sausages and flipping pancakes, Lola was setting the table and Brandon was playing with the girls. I felt like crying these people cared for me.

Brandon: "Come on in babe and sit down."

Brandon came over to me grabbed my hand and walked me to the table.

Tay: "Good morning sunshine, how do you feel sis?"

Tania walked over from the stove and brought me a plate and a cup of orange juice.

Tracie: "I feel fine, thanks for asking."

Tania patted me on my shoulder and winked her eye.

I didn't feel fine, I wanted to cry, I wanted to dye, I wanted to know why? Why did Kevin's son feel he had to hurt me? Does he know that his nasty trifling ass dad hurt me for years? I was so torn up inside. I couldn't eat, I couldn't do anything right. I couldn't focus. I got up from the table and excused myself without an explanation. I went back into my room and just cried. I decided to call my dad and ask him to meet me here at my home. Maybe I could get more answers from him. How could I put all that behind me, why couldn't I remember what the hell happened to me? Who was this Kevin guy? Why did it take him so long to contact me? While I was soaking in my thoughts I heard a knock on my room door and the door than open

Tracie: "Tania I'm fine I just need to be alone"

Brandon: "If I was Tania I would probably listen, but I'm your man so I'm not going to listen."

I turned my head and there was Brandon. I smiled to try to hold the tears in.

Brandon: "Baby I don't know what to say to you to make you feel better, but I know that I don't like seeing my woman down. You are too strong of a woman to let this take over you. You have people that love you out there and who want to be around you and just…"

I stopped him from speaking by sticking my tongue down his throat.

Tracie: "Make love to me Brandon."

He looked at me surprisingly.

Tracie: "Please Brandon, make love to me, no man has ever made love to me and I just want to experience it."

Brandon: "Baby they never made love to you because they never loved you."

Tracie: "Don't you love me Brandon?"

Brandon: "You know that I do."

Tracie: "Well make love to me."

Brandon: "Baby, right now you not well."

I kissed his lips and then his neck! I don't know why but I just wanted him inside me so bad. I wasn't up for sex but I wanted him.

He starts rubbing his hands on my nipples and kissing my lips with passion and love. I never felt this shit before, but I liked it. He laid me down on the bed and kissed me from my head to my toes. He kissed each toe and sucked them gently. He licked his way up to my thighs and slid my panties down with his teeth. I love this man! When he got my panties off he kissed the outside of my whole pussy, then he opened my pussy up and kissed the inside. Never have I been ate like this before.

He stroked his long smooth tongue across my erect clit. I moaned with pleasure begging him for more. He started sucking on my clit softly as his finger moved inside my pussy. My body started to shake and my legs tighten up around his neck. He looked up at me with his fingers still inside of me…

Brandon: "I want to taste you don't hold back, let it all out."

I laid back on the bed and spreader my legs wider. He went back down as he removed his fingers. He then stuck his tongue into my pussy hole and swirled his tongue around the inside. I couldn't hold it any more. I moaned louder as I experienced the most beautiful waterfall ever. He flips me over and spread my ass cheeks open. He stuck his whole damn face in it licking every corner and every hole.

I was shocked, never have I ever thought about Brandon during shit like this. He looks so damn innocent. I was so in a zone that I didn't hear him remove his clothes. All I felt was his huge gorgeous dick going inside of me. He stroked me slowly but deeply. I bit my lip to keep quiet but had a feeling that I was going to yell out so I grabbed my pillow and bit into it. Brandon grabbed my hips and rocked them to his rhythm moving in and out, slowly but deeply. I felt his dick in my stomach as he went deeper with every stroke. He laid me on my side and held me while he was inside of me moving back and forward as we tongue kissed. No man has ever made love to me like this, shit no man has ever made love to me.

He turned me over on my back and left my legs up,

he looked me in my eyes as he entered me, he stroked me long and deep and whispered to me "Tracie I love you." The feeling of him inside of me felt so damn great I couldn't respond back I just moaned "Oooh!" Brandon came closer to my breast while he was stroking me and laid his head on my chest "I just want to hear ya heartbeat baby, I want our heart to beat the same beat, for us to beat as one." I closed my eyes and relaxed as he took me to another planet. I had an orgasm that was so…words can't even explain! For hours Brandon and I made a union, we became one. I cried tears of pleasure, tears of joy that I finally have a man that loves me and I for the first time I actually love a man.

That morning Brandon and I just sat in my room and talked. I told him my fears and my goals. But, I could not bring myself to tell him that I fucked men and women for a living. We laughed and we cried. I was happy for the very first time. I asked Brandon to stay the night with me and make love to me again and again. I wanted to forget about my past and welcome my future. I wanted to start my life over and do the right things. I was going to leave the old Tracie behind and start on the new Tracie. But, I realized before I can do that I have to know who the old Tracie was and why was she so damn bitter. I had to call my father.

I got no sleep while Brandon was there all I could do was sit up and look at him sleep. I looked at my alarm clock and saw that it was 7 a.m. I got out of bed and went into the bathroom to brush my teeth and wash my face. I went into the kitchen and dialed my father's number, this time I let it ring. I was going to let it ring until someone picked up. But, I had no luck so I just left a message on the voicemail that said nothing just beep.

Tracie: "Hello Ralph this is Tracie your daughter, could you please give me a call back at 555-1229."

I hung up the phone and was walking back to my bedroom

then the doorbell rang.

CHAPTER 19

I opened the door and saw nobody in sight, I looked down at the ground as I was about to close the door and saw a package on my porch.

Tracie: "A gift for me?"

I whispered to myself. I went into the kitchen and opened the box. I screamed and ran out the kitchen. Brandon and Tania run out the rooms and met me in the hallway. Tania grabbed me.

Tay: "What's wrong Tracie?"

I couldn't catch my breath and I had tears coming from my eyes. Brandon looked me in my face and shook me.

Brandon: "Trace what happened?"

I pointed towards the kitchen and Brandon took off. I turned around to follow him with Tania on my heels.

Brandon: "What the fuck is this shit?"

Tania walked up to the box and screamed!

Tania: "Who in the fuck would do some sick shit like this?"

They both turned around and looked at me, but I said nothing. Tania walked towards the bedrooms.

Tay: "I'm going to call the police".

I told them nothing about the letter that was on the package that I saw after they left the kitchen. The package had no sender address nor did the letter say who it was from I opened the letter and it read…

"BITCH IT'S NOT OVER THIS IS GOING TO SOON BE YOU, YOU FUCKED UP MY LIFE!"

Why did this man hate me so bad! What the fuck did I do to him! He sent a fucking dead chicken to my house with the head of the chicken lying on the side of the body. The police arrived at my house exactly 5 minutes after Tania called them and I did not feel like dealing with them. I knew nothing and that's how I was going to keep it. This bitch Kevin is not going to take me down without a fight he caught me off guard the first time but not this time. I made it a mission to get a bigger gun tomorrow. The police took a report down and left the house. I was so out of it, I wanted to kill this bastard. Why is he coming after me, I should be coming after him after what his father did to my family.

I sat on the back patio sipping on some wine and listening to some old school jams, you know Luther Big Luther, Patti Labelle, Aretha Franklin, Al Green just some of my favorites. I could not erase that damn chicken from my mind. I'm so damn full of rage. I want to do some damage to this bastard. I was in my own lil twisted world thinking of ways to kill this bitch before he could kill me.

The ringing of my cell phone brought me back to life. I looked at the phone and it was one of my many clients Timothy. I forward him to voicemail and got up from the chair and walked into the kitchen to get another bottle of wine. When I stepped into the kitchen Tania was feeding the girls some peanut butter and jelly sandwiches, she stopped in her track when she heard me walk in and looked up at me.

Tay: "Are you okay babe?"

Tracie: "Yes, I will be fine, just a lot of shit on my mind."

Tania looked at me with a sad face and somehow managed to form a smile.

Tracie: "You will be fine the police will catch this bitch just try to relax and think about something that's positive."

I smiled at Tania and walked back out on the patio with my second bottle of wine in my hand. The wine was starting to get to me; everything started running through my head all at once. I wanted answers and I wanted them right away. I stared at my phone and then decided that I was going to call my father back. He has not returned my phone call and I wonder why???? He wanted me to call so damn bad but can't pick up the damn phone???

Why am I angry at this man? He loved me more than my hoe ass mama did and I hate him. Even after Tania explained to me what went down I still have hatred towards him. Why? I need to make an appointment with my shrink and this time hopefully I make it there. This shit was really starting to bother me. My phone rang again I hurried and answered thinking that it was my father returning my call but it was no one but one of my clients asking for some pussy and ass tonight. I told Louie that I would have to get back to him later because I was kind of tied up. He slammed the phone down in my ear. I wanted to call his rude ass back and go the fuck off but I just sat my phone down back on the patio table. I really think I'm done fucking all these strange ass men and women for money. I was in love with Brandon and I did not want to ruin that and plus this Kevin nigga got me shook.

Tania opened the door that lead to the patio and sat

in the empty chair next to mine.

Tay: "May I have a glass a wine?"

Tracie: "Sure go head."

Tania poured a glass and sipped her wine.

Tay: "Mmmmm very interesting taste."

I looked at her with a dumbfound look on my face.

Tracie: "You never taste Moscato before?"

Tay: "Hell naw."

Tracie: "This is the cheap shit anybody can afford this it's only like what $8 a bottle." Tania just looked at me and humped her shoulders while she sipped some more of her drink. I looked up at the sky and took a deep breath and started a conversation with my little sister.

Tracie: "Can I ask you a question Tania?"

Tay: "Feel free."

Tracie: "When I saw you when we had that argument you were pregnant, what happened?" Tania dropped her head for a second and then picked it back up and turned her head in my direction.

Tay: "I had a miscarriage after the fight that we had." I looked at her with a puzzle look on my face.

Tracie: "A miscarriage? When did this happen? How did this happen? O my God, was this my fault?" Tania shook her head at me while she sipped on some more of her Moscato.

Tay: "No Trace, it was not ya fault at all. It happened a week after the fight we had and it was from stress. I wasn't upset about it. I couldn't take care of another baby, I can't even take care of the two I have." She managed to do a fake laugh then start speaking again. "It was for the best, if I had the money I would have aborted it anyway but well, I didn't so it is what it is."

I felt like her miscarriage was my fault, it did happen a week after we fought. But, Tania did have a strong point she couldn't take care of the two that she had. That was sad and I felt bad for her for the first time. Tania poured another glass of wine.

Tay: "Trace can I ask you something?" I shook my head while sipping my drink.

Tay: "Why did you sleep with the gym teacher for $500? I have always wanted to know what was going on with you and the reason you would even think to do something like that!"

We laughed and sipped wine.

Tracie: "Well, I was 13 years old and we had no food no nothing, I had always noticed that Mr., damn what the hell was his name?"

Tay: Umm I believe it was Mr. umm, damn umm Mr. Frank."

Tracie: "Yea him, I always noticed that he was checking the students out especially me. So, I said fuck this, he wants some he gone have to pay."

Tania started cracking up. I laughed right along with her and continued explaining.

Tracie: "We was going through a hard time and I knew that at that time $500 was something mama could use. So, I gave my innocents to my old dirty gym teacher."

I did a depressed laugh, sipped my wine and held my head back up to the sky.

Tracie: "I felt so dirty the whole time he was humping and even though it was only for 5 minutes, it seems like it was forever. I was so ashamed at what I had done, I tried to scrape my skin off my body that night but the look you had on your face when I gave you that bag of clothes and shoes and the way mama eyes lit up when she seen that I had paid the light bill and the phone bill was so damn priceless."

I smiled and sipped some more wine and sighed.

Tracie: "Two months later I find out that I was pregnant and I couldn't dare break my mother's heart, so I, I..."

Tay: "You what Trace?"

I was still embarrassed about what I had done to get the money for the abortion, I couldn't tell Tania what happened that night but I knew that she was curious. I told

her this much so I should continue but then again, I

couldn't. Tania sat up on the chair and cleared her throat.

Tay: "Trace you can tell me it's only between you and me,

I promise I will not tell a soul and I will not judge you, shit

we all have made mistakes in the past. Shit, look at me I

start having kids when I was 14 and being going strong

since. I start doing drugs when I was 15 and was in and out

of jail. I was stealing money from mama and beating mama

up if I felt she disrespected me in any kind of shape or

form. Fighting you and dropping out of school."

We both laughed at how terrible Tania was when

we were growing up. She was a handful that's why I

always say that she killed off mama.

Tracie: "Tania why did you treat mama like that?"

Tania looked at me and then up at the sky.

Tay: "Cause of the shit she did to you."

I looked at her in shock; I didn't even think that

Tania cared about me like that.

Tay: "I hated mama for that shit I wanted to kill her for hurting you. Mama knew that you slept with that damn teacher, she never said anything because it was her idea."

I sat up in my chair and had a blank look on my face.

Tracie: "Wait! Tania what the hell you talking about, Mr. Frank wouldn't dare tell mama that he wanted to fuck me. Mama didn't know shit!"

Tay: "Yes she did! Mama always caught the way that he stared at you and how you was his favorite in class. She walked up to him after school one day and said to him I see how you look at my lil angel you want to smell that pussy don't you?"

I cut her off in the middle of her story.

Tracie: "Ok now, Tania you making shit up. How would you know this shit? Mama didn't sell me to a damn teacher for $500, shut the fuck up Tania."

I jumped up opened the patio door and stormed into my bedroom. I plopped down on my bed and said to myself

Tracie: "How much of my damn life don't I fucking remember."

I started thinking to myself why the hell did I get so upset at Tania? I need her, she knows shit that I don't even fucking remember. So, I decided to go back on the patio and apologize to her for snapping.

<u>CHAPTER 20</u>

I walked out my bedroom and walk into the kitchen Tania was sitting at the table with her head down. I took the chair from under the table and sat down. I grabbed Tania hand and she left her head up.

Tracie: "Tay babe I'm so sorry, I'm taking my anger out on the wrong person I do want to hear what happen."

Tay: "Trace are you sure because I don't want to get yelled at anymore."

Tracie: "I'm so positive, I need your help Tania because I don't remember this shit at all."

Tay: "I know that mama set it up cause I was standing there. You went to get your things out your locker, so you didn't know and back then I just didn't have the heart to tell you. Plus, you would have never believed me; you thought mama was so perfect. Mama got $500 out of the deal but she told Mr. Frank to give you $500. Her eyes lit up because she didn't think that you was going to go pay bills with your money. That's how mama knew that you slept with the gym teacher. That's how she knew that you did it more than once because every time she got a cut from the deal."

Tracie: "WOW, my own damn mama, the woman that I fucking cherished!" I couldn't believe what I was hearing I felt like digging her body up and beating the fuck out of her. My own fucking mama.

It was a week later since I found out the shit about

my mom and her prostituting me. I still didn't feel any better and my dad still hadn't called back. I decided to go back to work at the bank and going back to my clients. I had to get enough money to get the hell up out of Cali. It's too many memories here that I can't remember and some that I just want to forget. It's Saturday, Lola and I are hitting the High Rollers Club tonight. I need to get wasted tonight. Brandon tried to talk me out of going out then he insisted that he come with me just in case I run back into Kevin. But, I promised him that I would be alright and that I will call and check up every 30 minutes to an hour. Tania wanted to roll but couldn't find a babysitter and I was happy for that because I only go to the clubs for one reason and one reason only, MONEY! I wasn't ready to let Tania know what I did on the side for a living, shit I'm not that close to her yet.

I got out the shower and headed into my bedroom. I started applying my lotion and baby oil to my skin. My cell phone rang and I got up and walked over to the dresser where it is vibrating like crazy.

Tracie: "Hello."

Lola: "Hey hoe are you ready? I'm about to be pulling up in like 5 minutes."

Tracie: "Umm naw not really, I just finished oiling myself up just come in and give me like 15 minutes."

Lola: "Bitch!!! ok have Tay let me in."

I hung up the phone and instructed Tania to open the door for Lola. I got dress wearing my red D&B strapless dress and my red and silver stilettos. I walk out into the kitchen looking like a million bucks and feeling so. My face hasn't fully healed but it's nothing that real expensive ass makeup couldn't do and a good ass hair stylist couldn't cover.

Lola: "Ooo bitch you look real sexy baby!"

Lola loud ghetto ass shouted out as I walked into the kitchen. Tania turned and looked at me

Tay: "Damn sis you clean up pretty damn good boo."

Tracie: "Thank you ladies, I feel so good too. I'm ready to get my partying on."

I start dropping it like it was hot and laughing so hard. I felt good. I just wanted to put everything behind me and start all over. Tania pouted.

Tay: "I want to go."

Lola and I laughed she looked like a lil kid who was upset because she couldn't get any candy

Tracie: "Sis I promise next week when we go out I will pay for a babysitter for you and we all will go out."

Tay: "Okay, it's a date then."

<u>CHAPTER 21</u>

Lola and I walked out the door waving at Tania and the kids. About 20 minutes later we pulled up at the High Rollers Club and valet parked. We walk up to the door showed ID and strolled in. The music was banging and the men looked so fine. The usual classy rats were in the place looking for the cheese. I went straight to the bar and ordered the usual two rounds of 1800 shots. Lola paid and we down the shots and started dancing on the dance floor trying to spot out our victims for the night.

I was really starting to feel those shots. About two hours of dancing and drinking I feel an arm go around my waist my heart start beating through my dress. I hurry up and turn around almost falling to the ground and this strong dark sexy chocolate man grabs me with both of his muscle arms.

Dark Skin: "I'm so sorry mama I wasn't trying to scare you baby."

I smiled and caught my breath.

Tracie: "Um you just startled me that's all."

Dark skin: "Didn't mean too I just wanted to dance with you mama."

I had to gain composure of myself.

Tracie: "I would like that."

He started grinding on my ass, I could feel his dick getting harder and harder like he was about to explode out of his slacks. I bent over exposing my red and silver thong, he lifted me up and whispered in my ear.

Dark skin: "Let's take the party in the bathroom."

Tracie: "Not before I get paid love."

Dark skin: "Oh no doll, Mr. Deon don't pay for pussy. I can go home to my wife for that."

Tracie: "Well Mr. Deon won't be fucking Ms. Kitty; go home to your wife."

I proceeded to walk away from him when he grabbed me by the arm.

Dark skin: "Come on now love, you with this just like I am."

Tracie: "My mortgage bank want they money too."

Dark skin: "Ok, ok how much?"

He made his way over to the ATM and I went to go get Lola for back up. I was still scorn about the incident from the last event. I found Lola in the girl's room turning a trick herself. I looked out to see if I could see Dark skin and here he is walking towards the restrooms. I pulled him into the men's' room.

Dark skin: "Damn baby you want it that bad?"

I laughed as I pushed him into the handicap stall.

Tracie: "Money first."

He looked at me and shook his head like he couldn't believe that he was paying for some ass. He placed $500 in my hand.

Dark skin: "Drop to ya knees hoe and suck it like you missed it."

I followed directions as instructed. He began to moan, his knees started shaking as I swirled my tongue all over the head of his little, I mean very tiny baby dick.

Dark skin: "Suck that dick bitch!"

He placed his hand on the back of my head and begins to fuck my face. After 10 mins of sucking he pulled me up by my hair and pushed me on the wall.

Dark skin: 'I'm about to screw ya brains inside out."

He pushed his miniature dick inside my ass hole and begin to pump which I couldn't feel nothing. I faked every moan and scream just to make him feel he was doing something. After three minutes of him humping it was over with. He slapped me on my ass and told me

Dark skin: "Wasn't bad for $500."

I opened the stall door and Lola stood in the mirror laughing, while she fixed her makeup and clothes.

Tracie: "Shut up Lola."

Lola: (Still laughing mocking dark skin) "Say my name say my name."

Tracie: (Laughing mocking dark skin) "You feel that you feel it you feel it…. I wanted to say hell no, I didn't even know you were in me…"

Lola and I laughed all the way out the bathroom.

CHAPTER 22

We left the club and went to an after-hour spot called Monkey Bars to make more money. I ran into my ex-lover Sheila. A white girl who swore she was black. Sheila was a pretty high maintenance top dollar bitch. Daddy was a judge and mommy was a doctor. She threw money around like it was nothing. I was so happy to run into her.

Shelia: "I know that's not my black queen Trace!"

Tracie: "Oh my God Shelia, when did you get back in town?"

We hugged.

Shelia: "I just came in this morning, on a business trip...Hey Lolo."

Lola: "You know damn well my name is not Lolo it's Lola."

Sheila and Lola did not like each other and neither tried to hide it. Shelia would always fuck with her, but she knew how far to take it. Sheila knew Lola would beat the hell out of her.

Shelia: "My bad girl."

Lola looked at her and rolled her eyes

Tracie: "Anyway ladies, let's grab some drinks and chit chat."

Lola: "I did not come here to chit chat with ghetto Barbie."

Sheila laughed and I just dropped my head and shook it.

Shelia: "I see someone is still jealous of me."

Lola walked up in Sheila face and I jumped in the middle of them.

Lola: "Bitch of what?? Mommy and daddy pay for your shit you don't work for shit, don't get ya shit split in this club."

Tracie: "Okay ladies now ladies… Um Lola I see someone you may know at the bar, go say hi."

As Lola walked away you can still hear her talking shit and calling Shelia every name except the name her parents named her. I turned around and looked at Sheila and her face was just as red as my red bottom shoes. She was scared, she knew if I would have let Lola loose on her that would've been all she wrote.

Tracie: "I'm sorry about that you know Lola is kinda bipolar."

I was hoping she would laugh, but she just stared at me and forced a smile.

Sheila: "Um let's go to the little girl's room"

She pulled my arm and I followed… When we got in the restroom, Sheila looked under all the stalls and then locked the door. She pulled out this little sack from her purse and took a small tube from the sack and shook it on the table. A powder like substance came out. She snorted the powder like it was her last. I stood there and watched.

Sheila: (wiping her nose) "Come on girl take a hit."

Tracie: (waving her hands) "You know I don't mess with that stuff."

Sheila snorted another line.

Shelia: "Come on my friend."

Tracie: "No way."

Sheila stands up and walks over to me.

Shelia: "I know you, Trace and I know you love money…
You do one line and then let me eat you like a
Thanksgiving supper and I have a check with your name on
it." Sheila laughed as she licked my cleavage. I bagged
back holding her up so she wouldn't fall.

Tracie: "How much you talking??"

Shelia: "Well if you let my husband join us then I'll pay
you mmm… let's say four digits." Sheila starts laughing
and begins to stumble.

Tracie: "Where's your husband?"

Sheila: "I'll take you to meet him."

Sheila cleans up her mess, takes my hand and
headed out the club. I called Lola to let her know I was
turning a trick and where to meet me. With everything

going on I don't trust Shelia white ass either.

Tracie: "I invited Lola because I have never been out the city alone, I hope you don't mind."

Shelia: "Well, she can come too."

Lola followed us to this big beautiful house way out the city. We got out of the car and followed Shelia up to the wide porch. When we got to the door, a black, tall well-built chocolate man opened the door and greeted his wife; Shelia. Lola and I looked at each other. Lola leaned over and whispered.

Lola: "How the fuck she pull him?"

I elbowed Lola as we walked into their home. I thought my crib was laid out, Shelia house was amazingly beautiful. Sheila introduced us to her husband Cory who is a damn football player.

Corey: "Nice meeting you ladies."

Lola: "Pleasure is all mines."

I elbowed Lola again.

Corey: "Tracie, I have heard so much about you, you know Sheila loves her some Tracie."

Tracie: "Tracie loves Shelia too."

Corey turns and look at his high as a kite wife.

Corey: "So love, will both be joining us tonight?"

Shelia: "Well babe, I don't know Lola hates me."

Lola looks at Sheila and rolls her eyes.

Tracie: "She doesn't hate you Sheila."

Lola: "Don't speak for me."

I elbowed her again.

Shelia: "It's ok she might be afraid that she will like it."

Lola: "Anyway, you'll handle y'all business, I'll be sitting here waiting."

It was obvious that Corey had a thing for Lola. The way he looked at her is like he was undressing her with his eyes. He wanted her and if Shelia wasn't so high she could tell.

Corey: "Why not join us?"

Sheila: "Um babe, it's a threesome not a foursome."

Corey threw his hand up to shut Shelia up.

Corey: "The more the merry right babe??"

He turned to kiss Sheila.

Sheila: "Yea…the more the merry."

It was obvious that Sheila did not want Lola in the bedroom but she didn't say anything.

Lola: "No I'll just wait here and wait on my girl."

Corey walked over to Lola and kissed her as he palmed her ass. I looked at Sheila and instead of getting excited she looked like she wanted to cry. I had to do something. I walked over to Sheila and kissed her. A tear fell from her face.

Tracie: (whispering) "It's ok."

I pulled her little sack out her purse and handed it her. She walked to the bar and placed a line on the bar and snorted. She lifts up flipping her natural long blond curly hair.

Shelia: "Your turn."

I walked slowly to the bar I don't know what the hell I was doing I never did no shit like this before. But, Shelia always had her way with me.

Shelia: "It's ok just a lil snort."

I looked back at Lola and Corey hoping that Lola would save me but she was busy getting tongued down and fiddled by Corey. I got to the bar, moved my hair out my face and did one slow snort.

Sheila: "Yes baby, see tasty now ain't it?"

Instantly my body had changed. I got hot and felt extremely light. I felt the room moving in circles. Sheila moved closer to me and palmed my ass as she sucked my neck. It felt so good, better than ever, but I couldn't move. She took my hand and led me to the couch. All I remember seeing was Lola sucking the skin off Corey's dick.

Sheila pushed me down and opened my legs. I was in a dazed I couldn't move just smiled and laughed nonstop. She spread my legs open and took my panties off. I looked over at Corey and immediately got very horny. I pushed Sheila face inside of my pussy while I watched Corey pound Lola ass. This feeling that I had was a feeling that I cannot explain. I was on a high that I didn't want to come down from. The way that Sheila was eating me was something that I never had before. Before I knew it I came hard in her mouth.

Corey: "Baby, you and your friend come to papa.

Sheila grabbed me by my hand and hauled me to him. I couldn't feel my legs; it felt like I was walking on clouds. I was so relaxed. Corey stuck his tongue down my throat and I instantly came again as he fingered me."

Corey: "Damn baby!"

Sheila: "Taste her papa, she's very tasty."

Corey got rough as he pushed me down and stuck his long thick tongue into my pussy. I moaned for more. I looked around the room for Sheila and Lola. I spotted Lola bent over the counter doing a line of powder as Sheila slow

stroke her with the dildo. All I could think of was where the

hell did the dildo come from. Corey nibbling on my clit

focused me back to him. He lifted my ass up and started

licking around my asshole. I moaned louder as he stuck his

finger inside my ass. He stands up, yanks me off the couch

and bends me over. I screamed when his big black dick was

shoved into my ass. He whispered in my ear…

Corey: "Take this dick bitch, you like daddy's dick don't

you baby?"

I tried to answer him but, I couldn't. He felt so good

in me and the drugs was making me feel an all-time high. It

felt like the room was spinning, my body was numb and

everything was a blur…

CHAPTER 23

9 a.m. in the morning and we are just pulling up to

my condo and I see Brandon's car. I screamed at Lola in

panic.

Tracie: "O shit what is he doing here?"

Lola: "Bitch don't ask me."

I pulled my phone out of my purse and seen that he called 145 times.

Tracie: "O shit I didn't check in with him."

Lola: "Girrrl booo, so what, shit we was making money…lots of money."

I looked at Lola and gave her the stupid face… How the hell am I going to be able to explain this? I got out of the car and went into the garage door. I had some wet wipes in my purse I quickly washed my under arms, and all other parts. Sprayed on some more perfume and walked out the garage. I walked up to my front door unlocked it removed my shoes from my feet and walked up the steps I walked right into my bedroom and saw Brandon sitting on the edge of my bed.

Tracie: (in a nervous voice) "O hey babe you scared me

baby."

Brandon looked up at me with a look in his eyes that I have never seen before on him

Brandon: "Where were you Tracie? It's 9 a.m.!"

I walked in the bedroom and cracked the door just in case this nigga go insane; Tania will hear me scream or the gun go off.

Tracie: "I went to the club then we hit the after hour. We were too mess up to drive so we fell asleep at my girl Sheila house."

Brandon: "Who the fuck is Sheila? And still why couldn't you call me? No, no, no why couldn't you pick up the damn phone when I was calling you?"

Tracie: "Baby it's noisy in those clubs and my phone was in my purse I didn't hear it ring and I was well passed out at Sheila house."

Brandon: "Why the fuck didn't you call me like you said you was, I was sitting up here worried to death about ya ass and you out hoeing around."

I was so shocked that Brandon was talking to me like that. I had to stop what I was doing and turned to look at him.

Tracie: "You really need to calm the hell down, I went to a fucking club and I forgot to call. I'm not use to checking in with any fucking body. I am a grown ass woman."

Before I could finish Brandon jumped up off the bed and grabbed me; I just knew that he was about to fuck me up but he didn't he kissed me and looked me in my eyes.

Brandon: "I was so fucking worried about you Trace and you weren't answering the phone or calling and I just lost it."

At that moment, I felt sorry for what I was doing to Brandon but I couldn't stop.

Tracie: "Baby I forgive you."

I kissed him and told him to relax and make

himself-comfortable. I had to go get in the shower.

While I was in the shower Brandon creped in and got in the shower with me I figured that he would do that. I welcomed him in the shower with me. He kissed me passionately for at least 5 minutes. He went down in the shower on me placing my leg around his neck and tasting every inch of me. I came in his mouth so many times I lost count.

He stood up turned me around facing the wall and pushed me up against it, directed me to spread my legs and he stroked me so slow. I was feeling some kind of way a tear fell from my eye as he gave me long deep strokes. His speed got faster and faster. I came all over him. We exited the shower and just cuddled in bed. I've never felt this way and it was really starting to scare me. I put myself in some deep shit.

The next morning I decided to get up early get dressed and go order breakfast from IHop for everyone. I returned home and sat the table for the five of us. I walked

to the back knocked on the door where Tania and the kids

were Tania screamed from the other side of the door

Tania: "Yea?"

Tracie: "I prepared breakfast come to the kitchen."

Tania swung open the door

Tracie: "You did what, bitch is you ok you don't cook?"

Tania: "Shut up!!! Get the kids up and met me in the

kitchen."

I walked away and headed to my bedroom where

my lovely man was sleeping so peacefully. I crept into the

bedroom leaned over him and kissed him softly on his

cheek.

Tracie: "Raise and shine sunshine."

Brandon: "No baby, a couple mo minutes"

Tracie: "No honey, come on I prepared breakfast for us get

up."

I was tugging on the covers

Brandon: "Ok, ok. I'm getting up right now."

I grabbed his hand pulling him up. We strolled down the hall meeting Tania and the kids in the kitchen who was already eating the strawberry pancakes, fluffy cheese eggs, sausages, bacon, ham and grits. Tania walked passed me and whispered in my ear.

Tania: "How did you know that I love IHop?"

She smiled and I just bust out laughing. Brandon look at the both of us and wanted to know what was so funny but we just kept chuckling about it.

We had a nice little breakfast together we talked laughed and talked some more. Tania was laughing so hard her orange juice almost came through her nose.

Tania: "O my I haven't laughed like this in years, woo I forgot how it feels to laugh."

Brandon sat his juice on the table and picked up his fork to pick at his food.

Brandon: "Why has it been so long since you had a good

laugh, you know laugh is pain medicine?"

Brandon asked while putting a piece of pancake in his mouth.

Tania: "I just been so down and depressed I don't know what laughing is."

Tania put her head down and put a sausage in her mouth. I felt so bad for Tania. Tania is a beautiful woman she just looks so worn out. So, for once in my life I decided to do something nice for my little sister.

Tracie: "Tania how about I pay for a baby sitter and you and I go to a spa and to the mall then later we can go out to dinner or something?"

Tania's face lit up and she had the biggest smile on her face that I have ever seen.

Tania: "Trace I, I would love that!"

I smiled back at her.

Brandon: "How about I keep the kids while you two have a ladies night tonight."

Tracie: "Baby that's so sweet, you will do that?"

Brandon leaned over and kiss me.

Brandon: "I will do anything for you girl."

I smiled and kissed him back. Tania jumped up out of her seat.

Tracie: "Thank you guys so much! I'm about to get dressed right now."

I was happy to see my little sister happy. Strange huh! I excused myself from the table and went to get dress. About an hour and a half later I was ready to go. I met Tania at the front door where she was putting on her shoes that looked like she been had them for all eternity.

CHAPTER 24

First we went to my favorite spot Tricked Out Ricki's. I knew that he could work a miracle on Tania nappy ass head. I pulled up we went inside and Tay was so stunned.

Tania: "O my God Trace you get ya hair done here?"

Tracie: "Yup my hair, nails, massages and facials done here. They are great and the service is amazing." I pulled Tania by the hand and lead her over to Ricki's chair.

Ricki: "Hey diva how are you doing on this fabulous day my darling?" Me and Ricki exchanged kisses on the cheeks.

Tracie: "I'm doing all so good honey! I want you to meet my little sister Tania, Tania this is the best hairstylist in the world."

Ricki snapped his fingers in a circular motion

Ricki: "Say it girl!"

I laughed.

Tracie: "Tania this Ricki."

Tania reached out her hand to shake hands with Ricki, Ricki stepped back.

Ricki: "OH no honey we don't shake hands, we smooch baby you are family darling, come over here."

Tania smiled and kissed Ricki on both cheeks as he asked her too.

Ricki: "Now come on darling, sit here in this chair and tell me what you want done with this." Ricki started going through her hair with his fingers.

Ricki: "O my, what in God's name! Ooh honey, you going to need a lot of help with this darling!" He patted her on her shoulder and smacked his lips.

Ricki: "No worries honey I got you."

After spending three hours washing, blow drying, combing, pressing and sewing, Tania hair was finally done. Now she needed to get her eyebrows waxed and her lashes put on. She looks so amazing. My little sister was so beautiful. She really looks like something. I took her to the back to get her massage, nails and toes done. I have never seen Tania smile this hard. This made me feel good. Finally, we were leaving the shop after been in there for five hours. Next I had made plans to take her shopping at the mall. Summer Set Mall was my favorite. I know Tania

had never been there so she was in for a great treat.

About forty-five minutes later we pull up to

Summer Set. She looks pretty nice from neck on up. I had

to hurry up and get her out of these clothes. We walked into

the mall and we hit every damn store. I spent almost $5000

on my sister and my nieces and I didn't even get an attitude

about it. She was very happy and she deserved it. We were

walking out the mall to get to the car when I was spotted by

John and Lee the two brothers from the club that Lola and I

had smashed. John yelled at me from across the parking lot.

Lee: "Jane, hey what up?" I turned, looked at him and I

kept it moving quick fast and in a hurry. I was praying that

I got to the car before they caught up with me. Tania

screamed my name.

Tania: "Trace, damn wait up, why are you such in a rush

suddenly?"

I didn't have time to talk, so I said nothing just kept

it moving but if she didn't pick up the damn pace I was going to pull off without her.

Lee: "Hey Jane!"

The voice got closer and closer. Soon I hit the alarm on my car I hear.

John: "Damn girl if I didn't know any better I'll think you was running from us." I turned around.

Tracie: "I don't think, I know you sir."

John: "Jane stop playing babe, it's me John I know you haven't forgotten about me that fast. Shit all that dough I" I cut him off. I wanted to punch his ass in the mouth. This is exactly why I don't do city malls.

Tracie: "Umm sir, I don't know who you are, my name is not Jane."

Tania looked puzzled.

Tania: "Um sis what is going on?"

John turned around and looked Tania up and down.

John: "Damn shawty you thick as all hell mama, I'll love

to fuck the shit out of you."

O shit this ignorant bastard. Why he just can't get the hell on.

Tania: "Excuse me nigga?"

John: "My bad mama you a classy hoe too uh?"

I stopped him before he could go on.

Tracie: "Dawg get the fuck on you are disrespecting my sister."

Lee: "Oh, so she don't get down like big sis, uh Jane?" Lee came close and start rubbing on my ass. I pushed his hands off me and told Tania to get in the car.

Tania: "O hell no I ain't scared of these muthafuckers y'all got shit twisted. I will bust a cap in yawl fucking heads yawl want to play?" She reached in her purse and pulled out her 38. John and Lee backed up with their hands up in the air.

Lee: "Ok mama you ain't gotta get gangster on us baby. Jane didn't mind us filling her up two weeks ago."

Tania: "Nigga that's not Jane her name is Tracie, you have the wrong bitch naw get the fuck away from this damn car. Get!"

John and Lee scattered like roaches. We got into the car. That was such a damn close call. I pray that she didn't believe what they were saying. I have never run into any of my clients. Well, the married ones every now and then but I knew they would never say anything. I was hoping and praying that she didn't say anything to Brandon.

Tracie: "Tania please don't mention none of this to Brandon, cause then he will never let me leave the house."

Tania looked at me and grabbed my free hand.

Tania: "Ya secret is safe with me JANE!"

We both start laughing.

Tania: "It's ok to have one night stands sis don't worry about it, I have had a few of my own."

I looked at her and smiled and focused my attention back on the road. Something at that moment had just clicked to me, my little sister has always had my back even when I didn't have hers.

We pulled up at the condo and unloaded the bags from the car into the house and to my sweet surprise Joanne was there making the girls dinner. I really didn't feel like being bothered with Joanne and her God. I walked into the kitchen still smiling.

Tracie: "Hello Jo."

JoAnna: "Hey Trace."

Tracie: "Where's Brandon?"

JoAnna: "O he had to make a run he said he will be back later."

Tracie: "Mmm wonder why he didn't call and tell me."

JoAnna: "He didn't want to end you girls evening. I was stopping by to check on you and he ask me could I stay for a couple hours so he could go take care of business."

I popped a shrimp in my mouth that Joanna was frying and walked out the kitchen. I went into my bedroom to call Brandon to see what was going on with him. I sat on my bed and dialed the number. His phone went straight to voicemail. So, I tried to call again and the same thing happened I got voicemail. I was starting to wonder. I was getting up from my bed when my cell rang and I answered without looking at the Id caller.

Tracie: "Brandon baby?"

Lucky: "No baby, it's Lucky."

Tracie: "Lucky?"

Lucky was one of my ex's. Lucky and I was a couple through high school and a year or two after. I couldn't believe that he was calling me. What the hell? How the hell did he get my number? I'm not listed.

Lucky: "Hello sexy, you miss me baby?"

Tracie: "It's been what twenty damn years no I haven't thought about you boo."

Lucky: "Damn you are so cold, you still haven't got over the past baby?"

Tracie: "You left me when I needed you the most!! Man, how the hell did you get my number?"

Lucky: "I ran into Joanne today at the grocery store…"

I hurried up and cut him off.

Tracie: "Jo gave you my number? I don't want to associate with you Lucky, so please don't use my number ever again."

Lucky: "Baby, baby come on now let me love you."

Tracie: "Get the fuck off my line."

Lucky: "Wait Trace, I wanted to get something off my chest, just hear me out"

I sat there puzzled, as tears rolled down my face listening to Lucky talk to me about his affair with my sister. My trifling ass sister and the man who I was so fucking in love with. The man who I was supposed to marry. I would do any and everything for this bastard. We was together through all of high school, it's bad enough she fucked him then she got pregnant by him too. No, he just wants me mad. That's it, he mad because I turned him down. But shit only one way to find out.

I went and knocked on Tania door but I got no answer then I heard laughter coming from out the kitchen. I walked in the kitchen and Jo the girls and Tay was at the table eating the seafood that Jo cooked. I had a sit at the table and engaged into a conversation with them, really to Tania.

Tracie: "Tay, guess who I just got off the phone with??"
Tania smiled and popped a shrimp in her mouth.

Tania: "Who babe?"

Tracie: "Lucky."

She started chewing slowly and her head dropped.

Tracie: "Jo gave him my number without my damn permission, thanks Jo."

JoAnna: "Sorry Trace, I wasn't thinking I saw him and he was going on and on about you, I just thought that maybe."

Tracie: "Maybe next time don't give out my damn number

ok, thank you. Anyway, Tania he um…" I laughed about what I was about to say because a part of me believed that Lucky was telling the truth but the other half wanted it to be a lie.

Tracie: "He told me he has cancer and that he was asking for forgiveness to all the people he have hurt… So, this bastard tells me that my sister and he had an affair for over 6 months and that he has a child by you."

The kitchen was silent. Jo jumped up from the table and told the girls to go to their rooms. I knew by Jo reaction and Tania facial expression that it was something that I did not know. I could feel myself getting angry. I looked Tania and her face and asked her.

Tracie: "What the fuck is he talking about Tay?"

Her eyes formed tears. This bitch had a baby by my first love, shit my first everything. The man who I was going to marry? A tear fell from her eyes and she looked at me.

Tania: "I'm so sorry Trace I was going to tell you, I didn't know how."

Before I knew it, I leaped across the table and grabbed her by her sew-in.

Tracie: "What the fuck is you talking about Tania, you my fucking sister my fucking blood sister."

Jo came running in the kitchen screaming at me.

JoAnna: "Tracie let her go you will never find out anything like this, let her go Tracie."

So much confusion was going on, I didn't even hear Brandon come in the house.

Brandon: "Baby let her go let's settle this like some adults."

I let go of her hair and backed up. Brandon jumped in front of me and Jo went to rescue Tania like always. I yelled at Tania once again.

Tracie: "Bitch tell me it ain't true Tania."

Brandon was confused.

Brandon: "What's going on?"

Tay cried out as she stood up out the chair.

Tania: "Tracie I'm sorry I got pregnant by Lucky and my son is his. I tried to tell you but I didn't know how. I didn't want him to take you from me, you was all that I had. I didn't know what else to do Trace I'm so sorry."

Tracie: "How many times Tay?"

Tania: "Trace…"

Tracie: "Damnit Tania how many fucking times have you been pregnant by him?"

Tania: "My last baby was his too."

I couldn't believe what I was hearing. This nasty bitch! I walked around Brandon like I was walking out the kitchen to throw them all off and jumped over Joanna and socked Tania right in the face. I pulled her hair and continuously pounded her face with my fist. Brandon and Joanna pulled me off her and I backed up crying like a baby.

Tracie: "You is one heartless nasty trifling bitch, I fucking hate you."

Brandon grabbed my hands.

Brandon: "Come on baby you don't mean that that is your sister."

I yanked my hand from him.

Tracie: "I mean it I hate that bitch. Pack your shit and get the fuck out my house."

Brandon looked at me with a cold look.

Brandon: "Baby come on you are just upset right now that was a long time ago. Let it go that is your..."

Tracie: "Brandon stop fucking telling me what the fuck to do. That bitch gotta go and if you don't like it you can go with her... You probably want to fuck her too. That's why you always taking up for her and being so fucking nice to her Brandon. Huh huh Brandon, you want to fuck my little hoe ass sister?"

Brandon looked at me as if he wanted to slap my

teeth out my mouth.

Brandon: "How dare you stand there and talk to me like that. You have serious fucking problems Tracie. I'm not about to stand here and let you insult me like I'm some type of hoe ass nigga I don't want no other fucking woman I just want your stupid ass but you too fucking dumb to realize that every man not trying to fucking hurt you. I'm out... I'm not about to take this shit."

Brandon stormed out the kitchen into the back to get his things. Tania was leaking blood and Jo was cleaning her up. I yelled to the top of my lungs.

Tracie: "Get the fuck out my house!!"

I stormed to the back of the house to get to my bedroom. Brandon and I met each other in the hallway he placed my key in my hand and kept walking. I yelled out to him.

Tracie: "Brandon I'm sorry..."

He stopped in his track and turned around.

Brandon: "Trace I can't do this anymore, you don't appreciate a good man or appreciate when someone is trying to help you out. I'm done Trace!"

Tracie: "Please Brandon, I don't know how to love you. Can teach me?"

Brandon: "No, I can't you have to find love within yourself. You have to love yourself before you can love anybody else. I love you Trace but this is not for me baby."

He kissed me on my forehead and headed to the door. I was so heart broken. What the hell did I just do?

CHAPTER 25

I was wrapping things up at work. I'm headed to the door and my cell rings. It was an unknown number. Please let this be Brandon I thought to myself. I answer the phone and hear a deep masculine voice.

Corey: "Hello beautiful!"

Tracie: "Hello, who is this?"

Corey: "This is daddy baby."

Tracie: "This is not my daddy baby… So, who are you?"

He laughed.

Corey: "It's Corey, Sheila's husband."

Tracie: "Hello, Sheila's husband… Why are you calling my phone?"

Corey: "Because, daddy dick misses you."

I laughed.

Tracie: "Daddy dick is supposed to be for Sheila."

Corey: "Daddy wants you to get some more of this dick."

Tracie: "Not without Shelia."

Corey: "Ooh, I can make that happen."

Later that night Shelia calls me and invites me over to her home again. And asked me to please not bring Lola. I just wished they would squash whatever beef they have with each other. I mean they did eat each other pussy. I turned her down first, but after the millionth and one time that I called Brandon and he didn't answer, I said the hell with it. I'm not about to sit here and mope.

I pulled up to Sheila and Corey's home. Sheila greeted me at the door with a wine glass and a blunt in her hand. She kissed me on the cheek and invited me in. When I walked through the door Corey was coming down the stairs. I forgot how fine this nigga was. Damn how did Shelia end up with this fine ass brother. He flashed that gorgeous ass smile at me showing all his pearlies. All I could do was stare, trying not to be so obvious.

Corey: "Hello my sexy ladies."

I smiled as he took my hand and kissed it. My pussy instantly got wet.

Corey: "Would you care for some wine my dear?"

Shelia: "Or a line?"

Sheila bent over the bar and snorted a line or two. Corey poured me a glass of wine. Sheila signaled for me to come and take a line with her as she was playing with her nose. I wanted that high again.

I walked over to Sheila with my wine in my hand.
Sheila slapped me on my ass as I bent over to snort a line.
She held my hair back and I snorted. When I rose, I
downed my glass of wine. Sheila tongued me down pulling
my hair and gripping my ass. She turned me on like no
other woman has ever done before. My body start feeling
light. The drugs are kicking in. My pussy getting wetter.
Sheila, knocks the things off the bar, she slaps my ass again
and tells me to climb on the bar. I do as I am told.

As I climb on the bar I look over and see Corey,
stroking his dick as he lay back in their reclining chair. I
close my eyes as I lay on the bar. Sheila pulls my shirt up
and pulls my titties out my bra. Her warm lips wrap around
my hershey shaped nipples. I started to feel her wet tongue
flicker back and forth on me harden nipple. I feel her leave
my side.

I couldn't open my eyes to see what she was doing.
I laid on the bar stuck. Next thing I know I felt something

cold and thick enter my pussy. I moaned and opened my eyes. I don't know where this bitch got a cucumber from, but baby she was working that cucumber in my pussy like it was a real dick.

She twists the cucumber in me as she moved it back and forth, back and forth. I moaned louder, licking my lips and playing with my nipples. Sheila trace my clit with her tongue in slow motion as she pumps the cucumber in and out of me. She wraps her baby lips around my clit and make a muah sound, like she was kissing my pussy. I whined for more. I grabbed her head and forced her face deeper in my pussy. I swirled my hips in slow motion on the cucumber.

She slides the cucumber out of me, pushed my hips up and pushed her face in my pussy, taking her tongue sticking it into my ass hole. She moved her tongue in and out my ass. My body begins to vibrate uncontrollably.

Tracie: (Loud moan) "I'm... bout...I'm bout... Awwww...

I'm coming!!"

Sheila didn't stop. She moved her mouth back up to my pussy and sucked my clit gently as her tongue swirled around it making my clit pulsate. I came so hard all over Shelia's little pretty white face.

Corey: "My turn now baby."

He moved Shelia out the way and kissed her so passionately on her lips. He walked backed over to the chair, took his index and middle finger and signaled me to come to him. I got off the bar, pussy dripping and walked over to him like I was a little girl who was in trouble by her father. Corey was stroking his long, thick, chocolate, pretty, hard dick with his right hand.

Corey: Come have a sit on daddy's dick baby

I turned around and slid down on his magnificent dick. Corey's dick was so damn long and thick. He filled me up and had some left over, you understand what I'm saying? The man was packing and he damn sure knew how to use it.

Corey: "Bounce that big ass on my dick, you like daddy's dick, don't you?"

Corey grabbed my hair and pulled my head back. He kissed me aggressively. He starts thrusting his hips up and down, his dick pumping in and out of me as I bounced my ass on his dick.

Corey: "Answer me bitch, you like daddy's dick, don't you? Don't you, bitch?"

Tracie: "YES, BABY YES!!!"

Corey: "Take this dick then, don't run…"

Corey grabbed my hips and pushed me all the way down on his dick. He took his arm and wrapped it around my waist and stood up still inside me. He pulled out long enough to sit me in the recliner and spread my legs apart. He was back deep inside me pounding my pussy like there was no tomorrow.

Corey: "Shelia, baby come join in on this good shit."

I opened my eyes to spot where the hell Sheila was. She was sitting on the couch watching her husband pound the shit out of another woman. Shelia had tears in her eyes. What the hell happened? I thought she liked having threesomes… Why was she so teary eyed? Was it the drugs?

The way Corey was pounding my shit I couldn't think. At that moment, honestly, I really didn't care. Her husband felt good inside my pussy. Corey stops and look for his wife, who is now snorting a line at the bar.

Corey: "Shelia, what the fuck I say? Bring ya ass woman!"

Sheila: "Coming daddy."

Sheila makes her way across the room. He pulls out of me and walk to the couch and lay down. Corey looks up at Sheila…

Corey: "Come make daddy hard again…"

Sheila drops on her knees and start sucking the skin off Corey. I see his toes curl up and his eyes rolling around in his head. They say white girls can suck a mean dick, I know for a fact they eat the pussy just great.

Corey: "Tracie come let daddy taste you, ride my face."

I sat on his face as instructed. I bounced my big ass on his face. I literally fucked his face. Shelia made him cum all in her mouth and she swallowed every drop.

CHAPTER 26

We all got cleaned up. Corey went into their master bedroom and passed out. I was sitting on the couch, waiting on Sheila to come back down stairs.

Sheila: "Wine?"

Tracie: "Yes, I'll have a glass."

Sheila poured us a glass of wine and walks over to the couch to join me.

Tracie: "So, Shelia? What's going on lady?"

Sheila takes a drink of her wine.

Sheila: "Whatever, do you mean doll?"

Tracie: "I saw you tearing up when, you know?"

Shelia: "When my husband was fucking you?"

Something about the way she said "When my husband was fucking you?" didn't come off as she enjoyed the threesomes as much as he did.

Tracie: "Um, yes."

Shelia: "Would you wanna watch your husband fuck the shit out of another woman?"

Ok, now I was puzzled. This is what she liked. Isn't it? I looked at her confused. This was her idea.

Tracie: "Why do you do it then Shelia?"

Sheila takes another sip of her wine. She starts to tear up again. She throws her blond hair to the back. Sips her wine again. Looks me in my eyes and laugh.

Sheila: "To keep my man pleased…"

Tracie: "But, in the process you're hurting yourself…"

Shelia: "My mom and dad cut me off when they found out I married a black man. I can be friends with yawl, but marrying one and having babies is a big no, no. I love this man, I went against my parents for him. I can't go crawling back to my parents. They said he was bad news."

Tracie: "Did he start you on drugs?"

Shelia: "No that was all my doing… (She laughs) It takes my mind off all this shit."

Tracie: Do yawl have threesomes all the time?

Sheila: "Honey, we've never had sex one on one. Sometimes I just want my husband to fuck me."

She finished off her wine and shook her head.

Shelia: "I just want to make love to my husband one time."

Tracie: "Have you talked to him about this?"

Shelia: "I have so many times. He says it makes our love stronger (she laughs). He likes to see me sex another woman. But, I think it's his way of fucking without cheating. Would you like another glass?"

I shook my head yes. Sheila got up and walked to the bar to pour us another glass. I felt so bad for her. I mean shit, I fucked the shit out her husband. I thought she was all for it.

Tracie: "I'm sorry Shelia, if I knew this was how you felt, I would have never…"

Shelia: "No baby, no mmm mmm… I'm not mad at you and you owe me no apology. I just wished that my husband could see me. You know he only has threesomes with black women. We can never pull a white woman in the mix. Lord forbid if I ask him to sex another white woman. (She laughs and sips her drink)"

Tracie: "Seems like you both used each other."

Shelia: "Used?"

Tracie: "Come on Sheila, you have never been out on your own, mommy and daddy been taking care of you your entire life. You needed stability and he needed publicity. A sexy, white, young, and rich woman on a black hoodlum's arm. He made it, right? That's what half of these people think; that he made it out, because he's a successful football player with a white wife. He still and always will love his black queens."

Sheila looked at me in disbelief. I wasn't trying to put Shelia down, but come on now, she saw a gold mine and went after it. A black man, a sexy black man, with an education, pro football, and a big dick. Girl who the hell she fooling? Corey loved big black women and that was never going to change.

Sheila: "Wow, fucking wow Tracie! Don't give me this black king and queen shit. You really think that I went after Cory's money? I have money mind you."

Tracie: "No bitch, your mommy and daddy has money. Look boo, I am not trying to have you upset at me. I am just stating the obvious. Why, would you still be with a man who has no love for you? He won't even fuck you. You teared up when he was fucking me because he never fucked you like that. I am only telling you this because I am your friend. If I didn't care, I wouldn't even try talking to you after I fucked your man. (Sips my wine)"

Sheila: "Trace, I do love him. Yes, I want him to fuck me the way he fucked you. He wants you in a way he will never want me."

Tracie: "What?"

Shelia: "Ever since that night I brought you home all he talks about is you… How good your pussy was, how good you taste, how beautiful your smile is, how beautiful you are."

Tracie: "He really tells you this shit?"

Shelia: "No, I heard him telling his brother."

Tracie: "Ooh wow, I'm so sorry Sheila. I would never do it again, I will never come back around."

Sheila bust out in tears. I walked to the bar and consoled my friend. Lola and I was thinking she was living this lavish, happy life when she is hurting on the inside. She just wanted her husband to notice her. But, why put yourself through so much pain, heartache and confusing for a man who doesn't want you. To think about it, the first encounter I had with them and Lola he never touched his wife. Tonight, he never touched her. He likes her head game. But, why would Shelia stay? To prove her parents wrong?

CHAPTER 27

It's been 2 months since the whole ordeal with my sister and Brandon happened. I haven't talked to no one but Jo and I ignore her from time to time. I feel like it's all her fault, if she would have never gave my number to Lucky none of this would have come out. But, it is what it is. It's 5 p.m. and I'm just getting off work. I haven't been out the house in three weeks. Lola and I are supposed to do a party tonight, but for the first time, I'm not really up for it, but I'm not about to turn down no money. I already have something to wear so I'm about to head home taking a nice long hot bath and wait for Lola to pick me up.

I pull through the gates and like for the past month I started hoping and wishing that I would see Brandon's car and like before nothing. I park in the garage and walk around to my front door. I open the door and step in. I kind of miss my sister and the kids greeting me. I got use to coming home to a home cooked meal and company. Just when I was getting close to that sneaky bitch I find out she pulled some gutter shit like that. I went into my room and started preparing for my night.

I was dressed and waiting for Lola to pull up. I had took 5 shots of 1800 by myself. I had to get into the mood. I was ready to make the money but I wasn't ready for what I had to do to make the money. Sounds funny huh? I was always ready for whatever especially when it came to me fucking. My mind was still on Brandon. I have texted him, called him, wrote him letters and everything but I just couldn't get through to him. He never returned any of them.

I was so heartbroken. But I couldn't blame anyone

but myself. I was so mad I flipped out badly on him. The sound of Lola's horn disturbs my day dream. I got up from the couch and walked to the door. The 1800 was catching up with me. I locked up my house and got into the car.

Lola: "Damn bitch I see you started without me."

I giggled at Lola and then responded…

Tracie: "Bitch I'm just starting I got a gallon right here for us…what up bitch?"

Lola: "Bitch pour me a shot."

On the way to the party Lola and I snorted a line… Yes, you heard right. Since that night at Shelia's we couldn't get over that high we had so we got up on some. We drunk half a gallon of 1800. We stumbled out the car, now I was so ready to fuck anything that I saw moving as long as they had that money.

Another month had gone past and still no Brandon… I just gave up… I went back to doing me no feelings just straight fucking… I was putting the finishing touch on my outfit when I heard a knock at my door. I sprayed on some Chanel #5, grabbed my fur coat and ran to open the door.

Tracie: "Hold on Lola." I swung the door open and it was Brandon.

Tracie: "Brandon!"

He looked me up and down.

Brandon: "Well I see you have company my bad didn't mean to disturb you. See it didn't take you that long to move on."

He turned around to walk away.

Tracie: "No baby it's no one here, see you can come in."

Brandon: "Naw obviously, you was about to get ya grown woman on so…"

Tracie: "No Brandon, I was coming to surprise you. I was waiting on Lola because we were about to change cars. I didn't want you to ignore me if you saw my car. Please don't leave."

He stood there and looked me up and down again. He took a deep breath and kissed me like he never kissed me, like it was our first kiss. He pushed me in the house and closed the door. I had to make something up to tell Lola I knew that she was going to be pissed. I couldn't believe I was about to pass up thousands of dollars to be with this man. But, I couldn't take the chance of losing him. I pushed him off me to get the feelings back in my lips.

Brandon: "Tracie baby I miss you so much, I couldn't stand another day without you baby." (I'm fighting to get loose from him.)

Tracie: "Ok, baby look go in the bedroom make yourself comfortable I have to call Lola before she gets here."

Brandon: "Ok baby hurry up."

I watched him make his way in the bedroom and I went into the kitchen and called Lola. I told her that I wasn't feeling good at all and that my aunt Dottie had come to visit me (my period). She excused me and I met my man in the bedroom.

Brandon: "I love this little get up you have on baby. You making me very excited baby."

I had on a red sheer lingerie set with my stiletto heels. Brandon laid me down on the bed and kissed me from head to toe.

He spread my legs open and tongued my clit. I moan and spread my legs wider. I felt him flick my clit with his long thick tongue back and forth. He stuck two fingers inside of me as I moved my hips on them as if his dick was inside of me. My moans started growing and my pussy got wetter. Brandon started sucking my clitoris like he was sucking on a lollipop. He removed his fingers and stuck his tongue into me and swirled it around and around until I bust in his mouth. He stood up to unfasten his jeans. I got up and pushed him on the bed on his back. I slid off his jeans and his boxers. I dropped down to my knees, took his huge dick in my hands and licked all around the head of it. Then I stuck his whole dick into my mouth until his dick hit the back of my throat.

When I felt it in my throat I dropped my throat and slid the rest in till I felt his nuts on my lips. I then put his nut sack into my hand and start massaging them. I slowly released his dick out of my mouth inch by inch. I let my saliva ran out my mouth onto his dick and back down my head went. I grabbed his dick with my free hand and start sucking and stroking at the same rhythm. His body begins to tighten up and just to tease him I stopped.

Brandon: "Baby… baby why you stop I was just about to cum."

I looked up at him and I smiled.

Tracie: "I'm not finish, I'm not ready for you to bust."

I went back to doing what I was best at. I worked my way to his nuts and kissed them. I stuck his nut sack into my mouth and grabbed his dick and stroke it at a fast pace. I motor boat his nuts while they were in my mouth. His body tightens up again and I released his nut sack while still stroking his dick. His dick went back into my mouth and I sucked him until he exploded all in my mouth and I swallowed every drop and the drops that dropped back onto his dick I licked them up and swallowed.

Brandon instantly got hard again. He laid me on my back and opened my legs. He stuck his dick inside of me. It felt just like it was my first time with him. Soon he pushed inside of me I bust all over him. He held my legs straight into the air and thrust in and out of me back and forth. I couldn't control my moans and they turned into screaming moans. He fucked me like he was still mad at me. It was something that I could not take. I dug into his back with my nails. I marked up his back with my nails. I bit on his neck. I was never fucked like this. He never fucked me like this. He pulled out which was a relief for me.

Brandon: "Turn that ass over."

I got on all fours and he inserted his dick into my pussy. He slowly stroked me for about five minutes then it was pounding, hair pulling and ass slapping. I lost count after I climaxed 8 times. I got on top of him and slow motioned him for about five minutes. I had to gain control of myself back. I began to rock my hips harder and faster making the headboard shake. He placed his hands around my wide hips and directed them in the motions that he wanted them to move. I removed his hands from my hips leaned over on him and whispered in his ear.

Tracie: "No, no daddy mama's in full control of this ride."

I let my hips rock back and forth as I squeezed my pussy muscles around his dick. I start bouncing up and down as I held my tittie and sucked my nipple with one hand and caressed my clit with the other. I could fill myself coming hard I bounced harder and faster. My moans got louder and deeper. And before I knew it we both had an orgasm.

Brandon: "I miss that right there."

We both laughed.

Tracie: "Why did you wait so long?"

Brandon: "Because you needed that time to be alone and think about what it was you was missing out on…Listen, I'm not trying to toot my own horn, but I am a damn good man, and not only do I say that to you, I showed you. You always accused me of cheating and then with your sister? I couldn't take it no more."

Tracie: "I never meant to hurt you, but I have issues that I need to work on. Just be patient with me baby."

Brandon: "I came back didn't I? I'm here to stay baby?"

Brandon and I made love over and over. I decided to give up my ways to be a better woman to the man I loved. I wanted to try something new, I wanted to give love a shot.

CHAPTER 28

Lola has been blowing my phone up for the past two days. I have been slick dodging her because I know that when I tell her I wanted out the game she is not going to understand it. I finally stop getting nasty letters from Kevin the guy who beat me and raped me. I felt safe now that Brandon decided to move in with me and give up his rental home.

I hear the doorbell rang, I run to the door and yell

Tracie: "Who is it?"

I looked out the peephole and I see three heads, Tania, JoAnna and some old man. I open the door.

Tracie: "What do y'all want?"

JoAnna just walks in uninvited.

JoAnna: "Tracie no one is here to argue or fight, ok. We bought a visitor."

The old man walks in behind JoAnna and I then realized that this man is my dad. I stood there in shocked.

Tania: "Hi Trace."

I looked over at her and rolled my eyes. She had nothing to say to me. I haven't spoke to her in damn near three months.

Dad: "Look at my baby girl all grown up."

I stood there like a shy little girl! I didn't know what to say to him. Should I call him dad, should I hug him? What do I do? He walked up to me and gave the tightest hug ever. I hugged him back. We stood there hugging for at least 5 minutes, the tears started rolling. We let each other go, I wiped my face and we headed to the kitchen where I poured everyone a glass of wine.

Dad: "I miss you so much baby, I didn't know how to reach you, I always wanted to talk to you but you never, you never gave me a chance."

Tracie: "Well, I forgot a lot of things that this hoe, umm I mean Tania filled me in on."

Dad: "I heard, I was filled in on a lot of what's been going on with you."

Tracie: "I called you months ago, and you never called me back."

Dad: "I never knew you called sweetie, I was never given my messages by my wife, well ex-wife now. Anyway, dad's here now and I am willing to make up for the lost time. I'm sorry about everything that happened to you I tried protecting you Tracie, but I had to provide for my gals too, so I couldn't be two places at one time. I was planning on taking you guys from your mom that next year when I had enough money saved up, but I never made it to see it. When I got locked up that was the worst thing ever, but I don't regret it because if a mothafucka touch you again I would still blow they damn brains out. You are my daughter and I will always protect you."

My dad got choked up on his words he started crying, I was crying, Tania was sobbing like a baby and JoAnna was in the corner praying. We were so caught up in the moment that neither of us heard Brandon come in and when he did he scared the shit out of all of us. My dad was so startled he pulled his gun out.

Brandon: (With his hands in the air) "Wait a minute sir."

Tracie: "No dad, that's my boyfriend."

Dad: "My apologizes young man but next time make yourself known."

Brandon: "Yes sir."

Dad: "Nice to meet you…"

Brandon: "Brandon, the name is Brandon"

I walked up to Brandon and gave him a welcome home kiss.

Tracie: "I'm sorry about that baby."

Brandon: "No biggie love, let me go shower and change."

Brandon pulled away from me and faced everyone in the kitchen.

Brandon: "Hey, how about we all go grab dinner, my treat?"

Tania: "I'm down."

Tracie: "I just bet."

Brandon looked at me and pulled me to the back

into our bedroom.

Brandon: "You are not going to be nasty towards your sister."

Tracie: "I don't…"

Brandon: "I'm talking Trace… That is your sister your only sister, she made a mistake, that boy that she was with is now in your past, I'm here in your future focus on me and leave that shit alone, let it be sweetie."

I shook my head up and down. He kissed me on my cheeks and told me to get dress. Brandon took us to this Mexican restaurant downtown. We had drinks, food, we laughed, we danced, we had fun. I was back talking to my sister, me and JoAnna haven't hung together in a while and laughed and shared old stories. It was beautiful. I was happy. I had my dad, my sister, my bestie and my man. I was happy!!!

Joanna and I went to order more drinks while the other 3 cut up on the dance floor.

JoAnna: "Girl, I miss having a good ol time."

Tracie: (Laughing) "Me too honey, me too."

JoAnna: "Tracie, I am having a program at the church Sunday, and uh it's only me talking to women. Well, me just giving my testimony to women and telling them how I was in the streets and doing drugs... I would love if you just came to support me. Please."

I picked the drinks up from the bar passed her 2 and I took the other 3.

Tracie: "I sure would come and support you."

After we finished the few drinks that we had, we all went home. I got home, got cleaned up, put my baby to bed and I stayed up thinking. I am really starting to change my ways. I don't miss the fucking and dancing, I don't miss the money, between the money I had saved, my income and Brandon's income, I was set. I was starting to love my life.

CHAPTER 29

It's Saturday morning 10:25, and I hear banging at the door. I grabbed my gun from my nightstand and go to the front door.

Tracie: "Who is it?"

Lola: "Bitch, you better open this damn door."

I was not ready to face her. I opened the door and walked away.

Lola: "Oooh bitch don't run."

Tracie: "Nobody is running, I'm going to need a glass of wine for this."

Lola: "What the hell Trace, it seems like you have been ignoring me for a week now, what the fuck is going on?"

Tracie: "It has not been a week."

I looked into Lola eyes and could tell that she was stoned.

Lola: "Don't fuck with me… You made me miss out on money Trace."

Tracie: "How did I make you miss out on money.. I didn't tell you not to go do your thing."

Lola: "Cut the bullshit, you know I only do shit if you're with me and you have been dodging my calls."

Tracie: "You can dance and fuck without me, you don't need me there."

Lola: "What the hell is going on with you?"

Tracie: "I'm finally happy Lola, I don't want to mess my chance up with Brandon."

Lola: "Brandon, did you say Brandon? Fuck him what the fuck Trace we had a fucking pack. You don't ditch me for any damn nigga."

Tracie: "But he's more than that, why can't you see..."

Lola: "That you're in love??"

I shook my head

Tracie: "Yea."

Lola: "Fuck love, fuck Brandon and fuck you!!! You really dissed me for a nigga though and now you talking about you in love and you happy? You don't know the first thing about love, he just another nigga using your dumb ass, hope

he don't get your sister pregnant too and if he do, don't

come crying to me."

I put my wine glass down and walked in Lola face.

Lola: "What, you gone hit me big bad ass?"

Tracie: "Get the fuck out my house."

Lola: "Fuck you Trace, I been known you for a decade

bitch and this how you play me?"

I followed Lola to the front door. She went out the

door and slammed it. I knew that me telling her I was done

was going to hurt her but never thought it would destroy

our friendship. I decided to wait a few days to call Lola,

you know until she calms down, if she ever does. I needed

to get out my feelings, so I called JoAnna and my sister to

see if they could meet me at Ricki's to have a ladies day.

I pulled up at the shop and see Jo and Tania standing in the

lot. I decided to take a quick sniff before I got out the car

just to put me in a good mind frame. I sniffed some off my

hand and made sure no evidence was on my face. I exited the car.

JoAnna: "Oh my Lord."

Tania: "I can't believe my eyes."

Tracie: (Walking up to them) "Why do it look like yawl saw a ghost?"

Tania: "Are you feeling okay?"

JoAnna: "I have never seen you in loose clothing with flats on and no skin showing."

(Rambling through Tracie outfit) I had on capri pants and a t-shirt with a jean jacket… I never wear pants lets alone capris with a jean jacket.

Tracie: "Ooh you guys stop it, I just wanted to be comfortable."

JoAnna: "Are you comfortable?"

Tracie: "Very much so."

We laughed and walked into the shop. We got in the chair for our facials and our pedicures.

Esthetician: "Ladies would you like a glass of wine?"

Tania: "Yes, wine for all three/"

The esthetician walks off.

JoAnna: "Tracie, I'm so happy for you"

Tania: "Me to sis"

The Esthetician comes with three glasses of wine.

Tracie: "What are yawl talking about?"

JoAnna: "I have never seen a glow on your face. You have a different walk, a different talk it's just a different Tracie Burns."

Tracie: "I'm happy, I'm finally happy."

We toasted, we cried and we laughed! On our way out the shop we said our goodbyes and departure from each other. My phone went off as I got into the car. It's a text from a number I don't know. The message read:

"My sexy dear lady, I have let you forget all about me. I let you have your fun but time will come that you will face what pain you have caused! Be careful, be safe."

I knew that the message was from Kevin, I tried calling the number back but it wouldn't allow no calls. Why is this man huntin me?

CHAPTER 30

Sunday morning and Brandon and I are up getting ready for church. I have no idea what to wear I have never been to church. I wasn't ready for this. I wish I would've told Jo no. But, I promised her. She was so excited when she called me this morning. I'm going to go head and go.

Brandon: "Are you ready my lady?"

I turned away from the mirror to look at him. I stood there and stared at him as he adjusted his tie. This man was damn fine. The way he wore that black suite, I felt like saying no to church and yes to sex. But, Brandon wasn't going to have it, for he is a child of God da da da!!!

Tracie: "I guess."

Brandon looked up at me and walked close. He

grabbed me by the waist.

Brandon: "You are the most gorgeous woman in the world. God has blessed me."

He kissed me and led me out the room. We pulled up to JoAnna's church, as we walked in, so many people greeted us and welcomed us to this place. The usher led us to our sets as the choir begin to sing "Jesus I love Calling Ya Name" by Shirley Caesar and I sat there thinking back to when my granny use to hum this tone as she rocked and knitted. I looked up in the choir and saw JoAnna, and to my surprise, my little sister. I put my hand over my mouth in shock!

JoAnna spotted me out and elbows Tania to look, JoAnna started crying and Tania just smiled ear to ear. I loved the songs that the choir was singing; I loved the attention that the church showed to new visitors. I loved the feeling that I got from this church.

Pastor: "One of God's children is here this morning to give her testimony and her testimony is so deep that I asked her to share it family because it's someone in this church that has, went through, going through, trying to get through what she has been through. You see sometimes, God puts us through hell to pull us out and to share with others what we went through and how he helped us, how he brought us through, how he carried us, how he healed us and delivered us just to show that he is real he is able he is the almighty God."

(Church praising him shouting, screaming, yelling…)

Pastor: "Right now I want to ask Sister JoAnna to come and share her awesome testimony with us."

JoAnna walked up to the mic and began to speak…I sat there and listened, I related because everything she was saying about why she did what she did, the drug using, the sleeping around with different men was reasons I did it but never told a soul not even Lola. We did it looking for love.

We never had it growing up never knew how to get it, we did it to ease the pain that we suffer, we did it because we were lost in this world. I begin to cry, Brandon took my hand and squeezed it. I felt a feeling that I couldn't describe I felt a feeling that I've never felt.

She talked about God and how he changed her and I wondered to myself could this God they talk about do the same for me??? I want to leave my past in the past and move on to a better me, but could I??? I felt like this message was just for me. The tears would not stop coming. I held my head down and next thing I knew was a familiar voice that I know start singing.

Tania: (Singing The Battle is Not Yours by Yolanda Adams)

I stood up and the tears flowed and I don't know where it came from but I screamed and I shouted.

Tracie: "Thank you Jesus, Thank you Lord!!"

I didn't feel like me, I felt free, clean, I felt

refreshed. JoAnna came from the pulpit and hugged me and we cried and cried. Brandon stood there and prayed, he teared up and all I heard him say was...

Brandon: "Thank you Jesus, you got her."

Pastor: "God is calling you, God wants you, He is just waiting on you to come to him, He's waiting on you to make that change, give yourself to Him and let Him fight these battles for you... Come all God's children. God said "Come to me, all you who are weary and burdened, and I will give you rest." Come unto the Lord all his children, the door is open."

Something took over my body. I went up to the altar and fell to my knees. Brandon and JoAnna came up and got on their knees beside me. The church shouted. The service was over Brandon and I became members of the Church. After we signed up for member's class we met JoAnna and Tania in the parking lot where people was still chit chatting. We walked up to Jo and Tay. Jo hugged me so tight…

JoAnna: "I can shout right now Thank you Jesus my sister is saved."

Now it's Tania turn to squeeze me.

Tania: "I'm so proud of you"

Tracie: "Why didn't you tell me that you were singing better yet why didn't you tell me you was part of a church??"

Tania: "Well you never asked."

Brandon: "Say we go grab some food and have a big Sunday dinner? I already texted your father and asked him to stop by."

All: (In Harmony) "Sounds like a plan."

CHAPTER 31

Two months later, Brandon and I continue to go to church every Sunday. We had just came from church. It was our turn to cook Sunday dinner. Brandon and I went to the supermarket to get some food to cook for dinner and a few more bottles of wine. I haven't had a hit since yesterday and I was itching for one. I was hungry all of a sudden and start getting very irritable. I was so paranoid that Brandon knew that I was going through withdrawals. I had a feeling people was following me. I wanted to pull my freaking hair out. What the hell!

Brandon: "Baby are you ok?"

Tracie: "What? Why you ask me that?"

Brandon: "Because your very fidgety."

Tracie: "I'm fine, just hurry and pay."

Brandon: "Okay baby!! You sure you are alright?"

Tracie: "Brandon, shit stop asking me questions."

We get to the cashier and she's making conversation, as it is part of her job, but her voice was driving me crazy.

Cashier: "Hello how are you doing on this good Sunday?"

Brandon: "Blessed and you?"

Cashier: "I'm good! Going to cook a big family dinner?"

Brandon: "Yes we just come back from church."

Cashier: "How was service?"

Tracie: "Could you shut up and hurry up, shit."

Brandon: "Tracie!!!"

The cashier looked at me in shock, Brandon was more embarrassed.

Cashier: "How would you like to pay?"

Brandon: "I'm so sorry about that ma'am and card."

We walked out the store. I run out the double doors.

Brandon: "Tracie, what the hell is going on with you?"

Tracie: "Nothing let's go now."

I felt like I was about to explode. I was so paranoid; I kept looking around and clutching my purse like somebody was after me. I felt them getting close… I began to shake and rock as I waited for Brandon to put the groceries in the car. It seems he was taking forever he was doing it on purpose. I yelled out the window…

Tracie: "Brandon hurry the fuck up, what are you doing?"

Brandon gets in the car and slammed the door.

Brandon: "What the hell is your problem?"

Tracie: "Nothing I'm just ready to go, come on now let's go, start the car up and up we go, come on."

Brandon: "We not leaving until you tell me what's…"

He stops talking and just looked at me… I was rocking hard, clutching my purse, looking out the windows and tapping my foot.

Brandon: "No mane, no Tracie, baby what the fuck."

I looked at him scratching my head!

Brandon: "You on drugs baby?"

Tracie: "What the fuck, no now, no what the hell?"

Brandon: "We not moving this car till you be real with me. Are you on drugs Tracie"

A tear fell from his eye and at that moment I realized that I was hurting him as well as myself. But, this became a daily habit for me. I never skipped a dose. I needed this.

Tracie: "Baby, let's go please."

The entire drive home was silent. I felt bad for Brandon but I didn't know how to stop my cravings. I needed me a fix and bad. We pulled up at the house and I rushed out the car. Brandon got the bags out, while I broke down the door to get to my bedroom. I finally got the door open after 3 mins and ran to the back. I did not notice that Brandon was on my heels.

I opened my nightstand and pulled out a pink flashlight, well it resembled a flashlight. I shook some on my hand and notice that Brandon was standing in the door with tears rolling down his face. My heart broke but my body was craving this fix. I sniffed. He walked out the room. I heard my front door open, so I walked to the front…

JoAnna: "We here, my good people."

Dad: "Barely, Jo cannot drive."

JoAnna: "It was not that bad dad."

Dad: "I almost pissed on myself, it was that bad."

They laughed…

Tania: "Tracie, I bought ya niece and nephew to see you."

Tracie: "Hey babies."

That night Brandon was very distance from me. We ate a good meal now we was playing cards and drinking. It was a knock at the door…

JoAnna: "I'll get it y'all continue the game"

Jo answers the door and walks back into the kitchen…

JoAnna: "We have a guest."

Lola: "It's a party and I wasn't invited."

Tracie: "Thought you would be busy."

Lola: "If you'd call you would know I haven't been."

Brandon: "Lola, would you like a plate or something to drink."

Lola: "How sweet of you Brandon, a drink please."

I was looking at Lola, she was already drunk and high. I stared at her and she stared at me. My dad introduced himself to her and gave up his set. I went to get the chairs off my back porch, Lola followed me.

Lola: "I was wondering was my best friend ever gone to call me. But, I see she found her another bestie to fuck off with."

Tracie: "Lola, I'm not in the mood ok, I am not fucking off, I have changed my life around and that's that."

Lola: "Really? Have you? So why are you high right now?"

I tried to push my way through Lola to get into the door but she stopped me and pushed me up against the house.

Lola: "You know you miss me, you miss this pussy Tracie and you know it."

I was in total shock what the fuck is going on with

Lola.

Tracie: "Lola you high and you are drunk get off me right now."

Lola begins sliding her hand in my pants, I wanted to push her off but I was too weak. She stuck her finger inside me and begins kissing my neck….

Lola: "I love you why can't you see that, you should be with me."

I pushed her off me! Did my best friend just confess that she was in love with me?

Tracie: "Lola you are lit ok, you don't know what you are saying."

Lola: "Yes I do Tracie; I can't stop thinking of you I love you. I'll do anything, I just want to be with you. I'm tired of hiding it."

Tracie: "Snap the fuck out of it Lola, I do not want a woman I did what I did to survive! I love Brandon and that's who I want to be with."

I picked up the chair and walked into the kitchen. I walked in, Brandon grabbed me and kissed me. Lola walked in behind us. She just stared and I saw a tear roll, she wiped her face and sipped her glass. If looks could kill she would have killed me a 1000x.

Brandon: "I love you, and I promise you we are going to get through this together.

Tracie: "I love you more."

The next day Brandon put me in Drug Rehab 12 step program!! Brandon brought my sister, Jo and Dad up to see me from time to time. Jo brought my Bible up there and we read and studied it together. This book was my weapon. It helped me clean myself spiritual, physical, and mentally. I checked myself out twice and Brandon told me if I did it again that I would be single. It's been a rough road but 90 days later I'm home and I never felt better. Brandon came and picked me up from the hospital. We pull up to the condo, I was all smiles, I was ready to take a nice hot bath, lay in my bed and make love to my man. We walk

up to the door and Jo, my sister, her kids, my dad, some

people from the church and Lola jumps out and yells

surprise. I was so shock to see Lola, I hadn't seen her since

the incident at the house, but I was glad she was there.

All: "WELCOME HOME!"

Tracie: "Omg, you'll didn't have to do this."

Tania: "Yes we did, we are so proud of you baby."

Tania squeezed me so tight I couldn't breathe.

JoAnna: "Plus, Brandon threaten us all."

Everyone laughed…. We all went to the backyard

and blast the radio, had drinks, good food, we danced, they

even had a card game going. Brandon stands up and

demands everyone's attention…

Brandon: "Excuse me everyone, may I have your

attention?"

The crowd turns and looks at him.

Brandon: "Now, I have been knowing this beautiful lady

for about 4 years, she was, still is one of my clients at the massage parlor…

Tracie: "But, now I don't have to pay."

Everyone laughs.

Brandon: "Because she pays in other ways."

Everyone laughs

Brandon: "No seriously, I have been dating Tracie for a year now and it has been the best year of my life. We have had our ups and downs, but through it all I never had to question myself of her loyalty. She is an amazing woman; she is my rock, so I want to take this time and just show this amazing, beautiful, intelligent woman how much she means to me."

Everyone awe. Brandon walks up to me and drops to one knee, I put my hand on my mouth in pure shock.

Brandon: "Tracie Burns will you make me the happiest man on this earth and take my last name."

Tracie: (Crying) "Yes baby, yes!"

Everyone clapping and screaming…Lola slams her glass on the patio table…

Lola: "Are you serious, you saying yes?"

Tracie: "Lola please not right now."

Lola: "He don't even know you."

Brandon: "I know all I need to know, I know I love her"

Lola: "Do you really?? Do he know you Trace, uh do he?"

JoAnna walks up to her and grab her arm.

JoAnna: "Okay, Lola you're drunk sweetie, you had too much to drink let's go and calm down."

Lola: "No let me go Jo, you acting in front of all these Godly people, do they know your story."

Tracie: "Lola leave my house, you are out of line."

Lola: "Bitch are you throwing me out…well, before I go let me tell all of yawl who the real Tracie Burns is."

I tried to get pass Brandon to shut her damn mouth, but he wouldn't let me lose.

Tracie: "Shut up Lola."

Brandon: "What is going on?"

Tracie: (Crying) "Shut the fuck up Lola."

JoAnna tried to pull her in the house.

JoAnna: "Lola stop this now."

JoAnna was dragging Lola in the house and Lola

screams out.

Lola: "Brandon, your fiancée is a high price hoe, she has

slept with over 300 men and that's not including the

women."

I couldn't move, my body was hot, my legs were

numb, I looked around the back yard and saw everyone

staring at me and whispering, some was shocked and some

shaking their heads.

Brandon: "Tell me it's not true?"

I couldn't say anything I just stood there and silent

JoAnna: "Brandon, maybe y'all need to talk in private."

Brandon: "Tracie, tell me it's not fucking true."

Dad: "Okay young man, you don't talk to my daughter like

that in front of everyone take her in the house."

Tracie: "Dad it's ok, Brandon, yes it's true, but baby…"

Brandon pushed my hand from him and walked into the house… I followed him into the bedroom.

Tracie: "Brandon, please baby listen"

Brandon: "Listen, listen to what, you are a fucking prostitute Trace, you fuck for money, you a high-class hoe like she said, I should've known… I should've fucking known; can't no damn bank teller afford this shit."

Tracie: "Don't do that Brandon."

Brandon: "I'm out, I be damn if I marry a hoe."

Brandon walked out the room and shut the door. I sat there and cried for hours… I was embarrassed, humiliated, and heartbroken. I felt like killing Lola, why was she doing this to me. She is my best friend? Why would she do this to me? How am I going to convince Brandon that I have changed? Will he come back to me? What the fuck is going on in my life right now? Why is this happening to me?

TO BE CONTINUED.......

ABOUT THE AUTHOR

Takita C. Woodson was born and raised on the west side of Detroit, MI. She has an Associate's Degree in Leadership and Organization from Bethel University. Takita, is a plus size fashion designer and mentor. She started her own fashion brand called Vixenz Designs in 2015. Ms. Woodson started writing urban stories about the life of everyday people. Just something that many people today can relate to.

LIFE OF A B**CH PART 1 BY: TAKITA WOODSON

LIFE OF A B**CH PART 1 BY: TAKITA WOODSON

CPSIA information can be obtained
at www.ICGtesting.com
Printed in the USA
LVOW10s1755310717
543276LV00015B/1202/P